Wild Magic

Christel Jason

Contents

1- Master

E DON—

It wasn't the first time Master had left me for that long, stewing in my own filth. And I had no doubt it wouldn't be the last. He had a sadistic streak a mile wide, and he was careless, forgetful.... And I was forgotten again.

I flinched as I shifted, trying to take the weight off my wrists. He had left them tied above me, up high enough that my toes barely touched the ground if I stretched, and my shoulders and wrists had stopped screaming in pain hours ago, which I knew was a bad sign.

I wanted to cry in shame as my jostling caused my bladder to give in, and I felt piss slide down my bare legs. Since the last "showing", he hadn't let me relieve myself. He usually allowed me a few moments outside of the cage, with only the heavy chains around my wrists and ankles to keep me from bolting, after each showing, but this time he hadn't been happy with the money earned, so he had simply tied me up and left, mumbling and kicking at my cage. I knew he would be back. Sooner or later, whatever pub he had gone to would toss him out, and he would come back. He would come for me drunk, angry, and looking for someone to take his frustration out on.

And I'd be here. Helpless to do anything but take the beating he gave me.

I tried to cast my mind back, tried to think of anything that I could to distract myself. I immersed myself in memories of childhood. Of my ma, soft and beautiful, warm brown eyes watching me with laughter. My pa, his body strong and sure, so different from my small, willowy form. He had always assured me I would grow into my body, would grow out like him.

"There are no Carterson's that ain't thick as a tree, son. Someday, you'll be big as me."

I knew that at 20 (if that was my age; it was a guess on my part, really), I wasn't really done growing, but I'd have to do a hell of a lot of growing to be anywhere near my father's size. I didn't know how much of my memory of him was accurate, since I had seen both my ma and pa last when I was barely ten, but I remembered a mountain of a man, who dwarfed my thin, fragile mother. And I was barely six inches above five feet tall, with ribs that stuck through my almost translucent skin, and arms a grown man could wrap his fingers around twice. I knew that for sure, because Master did it all the time. I had the bruises to show for it.

It wasn't as if my size was the only way I didn't resemble my pa. After all, he was human. And I was... not. The gods only knew what I was; what they had made me. But human was not something I could ever claim to be.

It wasn't much longer after I pissed myself that I could hear Master coming. A few miles away still, but my ears caught onto his shuffling steps, lurching every few feet, and his frustrated, angry muttering under his breath.

Although I knew it was pointless, I yanked on the chains, rattling them against the cage. It was a futile attempt at escape, but my adrenaline had begun to pump through my body, and my fight or flight instinct was racing. Because I could do neither. I was completely helpless.

And Master was worse than he had been in a long time. I knew I was in for a long night, especially when I heard him come up to the cage and yank his belt from his pants.

I closed my eyes, calling up my ma's face, my pa's. I tried to immerse myself in their memory, and in the memories of the years after I left them. Of the furry bodies, the warmth of family, and the sense of belonging when I was with my pack. It worked, sometimes, to let my mind go towards these thoughts.

It didn't work tonight. As the first blow landed, Master spitting in my face as he roared at me about the mess I had made in the cage, on myself, the warm thoughts fled and I was left alone, a monster hanging in a cage, facing down a very different kind of monster.

2- Behold the Monster Become the Man

L HIAM—

The carnival had rolled into town almost a week before, and I had yet to bring Lacy to see it. She nagged me relentlessly, every day, but along with the carnival were the visitors from Kar'a, and I had spent every waking moment trying to fend off the advances of the Kar'a princess, Kalee. She was a beautiful woman, almost 12 years younger than my 30 years, and her clear, dark skin was a testament to the pure, royal blood in her veins.

But my frustration at her even being there shone through, I knew, because she was just another in a long line of women lined up by my council to try to get an heir off me. Ever since I had officially named Lacy, the daughter of my cousin, as my heir, the council had been frantically trying to shove women of marriageable, breedable age at me, and there was little I could do except smile, entertain the poor creatures, and send them on their way.

The council knew my preference for men, and apparently, they cared not. Stefan, one of my father's oldest friends, and the speaker for the council, had even confronted me about it just before Kalee's arrival.

"I don't care who you fuck on the side, Lhiam. You must marry a woman of royal blood, beget an heir, and then you never have to see her again!"

I didn't know if there was something broken inside of me, because none of the council members or their wives seemed to have a problem with the idea, but even the thought of marrying someone who didn't appeal to me, and then never seeing them except to breed them, made bile rise in my throat.

I couldn't do it. And if not marrying someone I could truly care for, be attracted to, meant I would be alone for the rest of my life, then so be it. I would bear that rather than live a life that made me want to vomit everything I had eaten.

The morning the princess of Kar'a left, her disappointment at my refusal to her advances obvious, Lacy sought me out, and I knew I would have no choice but to take her down to the village.

My kingdom is small, but we are wealthy. Teren is one of seven kingdoms that make up the Wer'ren Empire, of which Kar'a is another kingdom. Each kingdom is ruled by a prince, all answering to the Emperor. I was little more than a figurehead; my line had been for a long time. The Emperor made the state decisions, I followed through with them. It was something I was comfortable with, because the Emperor had never been a cruel master to serve. His taxes were fair, and his law just, never mind our personal relationship— we'd been friends since childhood. Emperor Riece at the helm left me free for projects I would rather spend my time on. Like the school I had started in the village just below my keep, or the daily rations I had Chef prepare for the homeless, widows, and orphans. The things my council called a waste of time, frivolous, feminine pursuits. Those were the things I wanted to spend my life doing, damn the men on the council. I had wasted enough of my life fighting wars my father sent me to fight, killing men my father sent me to kill. I wanted to spend the rest of it doing something that actually meant something.

And if that meant I was mocked as feminine and soft behind my back, so be it. I had more than proven myself capable on the battlefield, and none of the men who spoke ill of me would dare face me with a sword in my hands.

I allowed Lacy to drag me to town, and into the chaos of the festival. I spent the entire day being dragged from one cart and table to another, from psychics to mystics, to animals doing amazing tricks.

Lacy was my late-cousin's daughter. My cousin, who had been raised as something like a sister to me, had died giving birth to Lacy. Tragically, Lacy's father was killed in a sea raid as he made his way back from a diplomatic meeting at the Emperor's palace— coming back to meet Lacy, and to be with his wife during labor.

The moment I had looked into the bassinet holding my little cousin 12 years ago, she had wrapped me around her tiny finger and I had never been the same. She was more my daughter than my cousin, although as she got older our relationship had evolved into siblings rather than father and daughter. She was my everything.

I was exhausted beyond belief by the time the sun set, but Lacy wasn't flagging. I began to beg her, wanting nothing more than a large bowl of stew and my warm bed, but she made me promise one more stop. I dragged my feet and she laughed, yanking on my arm to carry me toward the last cart. It was at the end of all the others, out of the light from the bonfire in the center of town. There was a small cage, barely large enough to hold a man crouched down, that lay next to a dilapidated cart, with an old donkey grazing nearby. The cage had some sort of tarp hanging over it, covering all but four large, dirty paws. The creature, possibly a dog, had chains around all four paws, but I could see nothing else for the tarp.

A large, flabby man stepped out from behind the cage just as Lacy and I joined the crowd around the cage. The crowd was small and quiet. All watched the man, looking from him to the cage and back again.

"Prepare!" the man yelled, his theatrical, fake-scared voice carrying around the small clearing around us. "Prepare to see magic, before your very eyes. Prepare to see a monster turn into a man. Or is it a man who turns into a monster!"

I raised my brows, amused as Lacy gripped at my hand, her fingers shaking in mine.

"Lhiam," she whispered, unsure. I squeezed her hand back, reassuring her, and met Tate's eyes across the crowd. My constant guard, and friend, saw Lacy's reaction with the same amusement I did, but when his eyes met mine, and they flicked to the cage, there was something else there. Something hesitant, and angry.

I glanced back over at the cage just as the man yanked the tarp from the top. Inside was a small wolf. Dark gray, almost completely black, it had a few light gray, almost white spots on its belly and near its muzzle. I momentarily wondered if they would be white if he were cleaner, because gods, the animal was disgusting. Its fur was matted, and now that the tarp was removed, it smelled so strongly of urine and other unpleasant smells that not a few noses were plugged as a gasp went through the crowd.

"Behold, the monster!" the man cried, a smirk on his face as the wolf cowered in the corner, the chains rattling as it ducked its head. I could see now that it not only had chains around its four paws, but it had a metal collar around its neck as well.

It was small for a wolf, looking more like a large dog, and it was underfed. I could visibly see the animal's ribs through its ratted fur.

But the wolf's eyes. Gods, its eyes met mine for only a moment before the man moved and it cowered again, but as it did, a jolt of something went through my entire body. Something like knowing. Like understanding.

Something like recognition.

But then the huge amber eyes had closed as the man jabbed a rod at the cage, poking at its ribs. It yelped, baring its teeth feebly, and the man chuckled.

"Now see the man," he finished, and all the breath in the crowd seemed to exit at once as everyone leaned forward. The moon was just beginning to rise above the trees to the east when the wolf looked up at the man, its disapproval and glare obvious. I smiled, silently cheering at its defiance, but the man wasn't as amused as I. He jabbed the rod into the wolf a few more times, my hand in Lacy's getting tenser and tenser with each jab. But there was little I could do. The man wasn't even one of my subjects, and it was a wild animal. There were no laws against what he was doing.

That didn't make me any less furious as I almost unconsciously began to move forward to stop him. But just as I reached the front of the crowd, Lacy's hand in mine so tight around me I knew her anger was as fierce as my own, the wolf began to twitch. It yelped, leaping back, and the man finally turned to the crowd.

"Behold, the monster become the man!"

The twitching, yelping wolf spasmed, and in what felt like the blink of an eye, in its place crouched a man. Well, more a boy. He was in his late teens at most, completely coated in filth, his nearly translucent skin pasty. His bones pressed out of his skin, obviously malnourished and starving, and his thick, black hair hung in chunks around his face. He crouched with his arms around his knees, his face nearly completely obscured by his matted hair. He was naked and he tried to cover himself the best he could, but I could see him shiver in the cold autumn wind.

My breath left me in a rush, as the same deja vu sense of knowing I had felt before hit me again. I gasped, rage rushing through my blood like a fire.

"What the fuck is this?" I hissed. The boy flinched, his eyes shutting against my anger, and I tried to calm myself. Especially when I noticed the chains wrapped around his ankles, wrists and neck. I had seen them on the wolf, but a new sort of rage went through me, seeing them on the boy. Because beneath the chains were heavy bondage scars, likely from years and years of those chains cutting into his thin skin.

And those had me seeing red in the worst way. I yanked my hand from Lacy's grip, barely registering Tate stepping up behind me to stand beside my cousin.

"M'lord," the man began, as the crowd around him, all of whom knew who I was, began to disperse, chagrined.

"Slavery is illegal in this region," I growled, flinching as the boy scrabbled back, away from me. "You must have been aware of this. It has been made illegal in all of the kingdoms in the Empire."

"M'lord, it's not human. It ain't slavery if it—"

"Silence," I hissed, trying to keep my voice as calm as I could. I could tell we were terrifying the boy. "I am Prince Lhiam of Teren. You will release the boy into the custody of my man. We will pay you twenty gold pieces, for your loss of revenue, and you'll be grateful that I don't simply free him and leave you out the money, which I am in my rights to do."

The man's gasp of anger was cut short by Tate stepping up behind me and shoving a bag of gold into his hands.

"Most appreciated, your highness," he muttered under his breath, glaring at the bag.

I nodded, only then noticing the boy's eyes on me. They were bright, as if with fever. They were most definitely the same huge, amber eyes of the wolf, and they watched me with the same wild cunning the wolf had.

I turned on my heel, grabbing Lacy's hand again, and heading towards the keep. Tate would bring the boy. And I had shown enough emotion in front of a crowd of my subjects for one day.

3- Like Fire

EDON—

Master gave me only an hour after my beating before I heard his voice, extolling the monster. When the tarp was yanked from the cage, I was blinded by the sights and sounds around me. So many people, far too many, surrounded my cage. I could feel the surprise, excitement, and curiosity.

And then, by all the gods, the rage. It hit me like one of Master's sticks, right in the gut. And it amplified as I shifted, my bones realigning into the shape of man.

As the anger moved towards me, so did a man. He was tall and at least double my size. He wasn't particularly muscled, but he was firm, his arms bulging as he glared me down. His eyes flashed from me to Master, his words jumbling with Master's. I had learned long ago to tune out the words of men. They were so very rarely words I wanted to hear. They were usually filled with anger. With disgust. With venom.

So I unlearned how to speak, how to listen. But something about this man made me want to understand again. I feared I had lost the ability to hear the words of men, for his words continued to roll off of my body like water, even as I tried to concentrate.

His ire rolled off of him in waves, and my body cowered away from it instinctively, trying to protect my soft belly and groin, just in case he came at me. But he never did. With a few final words, he turned on his heel, leaving me alone with Master and another man. The second man smelled of blood, and sweat, and work. He smelled of leather, and steel, and a blacksmith's forge.

He smelled like fire.

That man lifted the tarp back over my cage, and I was left in the dark. I shifted back to my wolf, because it was warmer with fur coating me, rather than only my thin human skin. It was only a few minutes later that I felt the cage lift, and then the clatter of hooves as I was dragged somewhere. I tucked myself into as tight a ball as I could, unsure where I was being taken, but uncaring. One cage was the same as another. One Master the same as another.

Hopefully this one wouldn't touch me, force himself inside me, like my last one, the one before my current master. Like the men Master sold my body to. I shivered, forcing those thoughts from my mind. I couldn't think of him, of them. I couldn't think of that time. It was too dark, and I would lose myself again. Like I had when I first left my family. I would lose myself to my wolf, and Edon the man would die.

Just like before.

We rode up for what felt like hours, but may have only been minutes, before the cart stopped, the horse's hooves quieted, and the man who smelled of fire was gone. He took with him the horse and cart, and my cage was lowered to the ground. For a few minutes, I wondered if I had been forgotten. If maybe they would just leave me alone. Let me fade away in this cage.

But no. Of course not. Because humans were never that kind.

Before long, there was the sound of boots in grass, and then the smell of a warm fire, parchment, and ink. The tarp was yanked from the cage, and I looked around quickly, assessing my surroundings. It wouldn't be the first time my master had lent me out for the night, but usually that meant I was tied to Master's bed in his cart, and the man, or men, who bought me were given an hour. Master had never allowed me to be taken somewhere else like this.

I was in a clearing, some kind of garden. A stone wall surrounded it, and my wolf immediately whined in pain at being caged in even further. My cage sat atop thick, green grass, and before me stood the tall, angry man. His anger seemed to have abated for now. He watched me with a face of stone, not showing any emotion. But I could smell it. He was confused, curious, and hesitant. But most of all, he was sad. Upset.

But at least he was no longer angry.

He began to speak, but I ignored him, praying to any gods listening that he would make it quick. If he wanted me to shift into a man so he could press himself inside me, I would fight. As I always did. But even as the thought entered my mind, I wanted to laugh. Yes, I always fought. But it never stopped them. And I was a coward. I was only ever able to hold out until the pain became too much before I gave in.

I always gave in.

The man quieted after a while, and I reveled in the relative silence that surrounded us. It was almost peaceful. I could almost make myself believe that I was somewhere safe. Warm. Somewhere like home.

But then he was talking again, and I looked up into icy blue eyes. His eyes were the color of a glacier in the sun, and they shone with a sort of warm intelligence I had never seen before. They drew me to him, and I would have gasped if I had the throat for it. As it was, I chuffed softly, my shivering increasing as the man stared me down.

He was sitting cross-legged on the ground, his rich clothes getting dirty from the damp dirt beneath the grass. His hands were limp in his lap, but when I continued to study him, he clenched them a bit, as if self-conscious of my perusal.

His voice was soft, deep, and warm. I closed my eyes, concentrating on the cadence of his speech. I jumped and yelped when I heard the lock disengage, and then his words became a question as he opened the door. I flinched back into the corner, fear eating at me.

I didn't want him to touch me. Gods, I wanted, for once, to scream, to rage, to fight against the pain he would surely soon bring me.

But I didn't. I simply watched, and waited, like the coward I am, as the man sat back again once the door to the cage was open. And while I knew it was ridiculous, I couldn't stop the idea forming that I could run past him, maybe even make it to the freedom I knew waited beyond those damned stone walls.

The man held his hand out, and my eyes went directly to it, almost of their own accord. I kept myself from flinching back, expecting a backhand, but he simply held his hand out, speaking in his deep, rhythmic voice.

Gods, what did he want?

I concentrated, forcing all other thoughts back except what this man was saying. Everything except what he was rattling off as he held his hand out to me. And finally, finally, he began to make a sort of sense.

"Safe..." he paused, cocking his head as I met his eyes again. Maybe he saw my concentration there, maybe he saw that I understood now. Maybe he just ran out of breath. But he froze, staring me down, and then he smiled.

And gods, what a smile. I took two unconscious steps towards him, staring at that smile, before I stopped myself, horrified.

I shook my head, chuffing out and glaring him down. His smile widened and he snorted. "Don't give me that look," he laughed, and I mentally patted my own back. It was the first time I understood a human's words in years. The first time I listened for words from their mouths, rather than only trying to guess at where the next blow would land.

"You're safe, little one," he began again, his hand still held out, steady. "I won't hurt you. No one here will. You're safe. I would really like to get those damn... those chains off. But I have to know you're not going to go for my face. Tate wouldn't be happy with me if I got permanently scarred by a wolf. I think I'd look rather dashing with claw marks down my face, but it might scare off..."

I snorted, shaking my head as I took another step towards him. Surely he was lying about taking the chains off. Surely it was some trick to get me to give myself up to him. To trust him. And then he would show himself for the monster he was.

The monster they all turned out to be, one way or another.

"I know you've been hurt, little one. I know you don't know if you can trust me. I have nothing to show you, nothing I can give you to prove myself. I can only do that with time. But please. They are hurting you, and it's hurting me to see how much. Please. I have the key. Let me take them off. I want to help you. I want to get a doctor for you, a healer. I know you're in pain. I can see the injuries. Some are damn new, from what I can tell.

"Let me help you," he whispered, his hand wavering as he spoke. I took a few more steps forward, lowering my belly to the ground and tilting my head in submission. I prayed he was telling the truth and would really take the chains off, but that was all I could do: hope and pray. There was nothing I could do if he lashed out instead, as I suspected he would.

I whined, my entire body shaking as I pushed myself under his hand and then stilled. He froze for a moment, and then I felt his hands on my fur. They were so warm, I wanted to press myself against him. I hadn't even known how cold I was until I felt his hot skin against me.

He moved slowly, unlocking first my front paws, then my back, and finally my neck. When the collar fell to the grass, I felt a wave of anger pour from the man, and it was all I could do to hold myself back from leaping away from him. I froze, an occasional spasm the only move I made, as his fingers explored my neck.

"Fuck," he hissed, and I whined, terrified at the rage in his voice. "No, little one," he murmured, and I felt a soothing calm fall over me, making me want to roll onto my back, exposing my belly in total surrender. "I'm not angry with you, sweet one. The damn collar had spikes. The injuries have festered; they're infected. I really need to get a doctor for you."

I growled, and he froze. One man was bad enough. Two would be able to overpower me with ease. Hold me down as they took turns, like so many before had.

"That's alright. We can wait. I'm sure, if you're still alive after it being that way for this long, that you'll survive a while longer."

I huffed out a breath, pulling my back legs down so I was lying next to the man. His hand hadn't left my neck yet, and that warm wave of calm came over me again as he dug his fingers into my fur.

"Gods, you're beautiful," he whispered, gently petting my neck, careful to keep his hands off of my injuries.

I chuffed, trying to warn him.

I'm dirty. Don't dirty your hands on me.

But he didn't seem to understand, and I couldn't remember the last time I had spoken, even if I did shift into my human form. I didn't even know if I could still speak.

He was quiet for a few more minutes, before he stirred. I hissed and leapt back, away from the cage, and he froze.

"Sorry," he mumbled, a blush spreading across his cheeks as he motioned at his legs. "My legs were falling to sleep."

His eyes were heavy on me as I looked from him to the gate behind him. I could smell open air behind that gate, and I knew that beyond it was my freedom. Liberation, or death. Either way, I was free.

He seemed to understand my thoughts, because his eyes darkened with a heavy sadness. "Go, if you want to," he whispered, his words so soft I barely heard them. I tilted my ears towards him, wanting to catch every nuance of his voice. "I won't hold anyone prisoner. But I don't think you'll survive long if you go. At least let me get you healed up, and fed, before you go. I promise you, if you trust me, just for a while, you can leave anytime you want. I'll never keep you against your will."

I lowered my body to the ground again, mostly out of exhaustion. I wanted so much to believe his words. To believe that he wouldn't hurt me; that I was safe; that he cared. But past experience was a difficult thing to move past, and it was screaming at me to run, to fight, to escape. Before he had a chance to touch me; before he had a chance to hurt me. And there was a nagging in the back of my mind that told me that this human, this man, would be able to rip me open in ways none of the men in my past had. That he would be able to truly break me, as I had fought against for so long.

But I couldn't run. Even if he did let me go, like he said he would, I knew I wouldn't make it far. I was weak from starvation, and from the beating I had taken earlier in the day. And I was damn tired. I just wanted to sleep. To fall into the black, and never to wake.

But the gods were cruel.

So I trusted. For the first time in so, so long, I trusted a human.

And I could only hope he wouldn't make me regret it.

4- Grip Me Back

LHIAM—

When I offered his freedom, I thought the poor creature was going to have a heart attack. His eyes flicked from me, to the gate behind me, and back again. I could feel my fury at the man who had hurt him boiling just under my skin, but I held it at bay. I had to care for him now, and every time I had allowed my anger to show, it had affected him. I had to keep myself calm.

When I first came into the garden and saw him cowering in the cage, it took everything in me not to rip the door open and yank him out and into my arms. He looked so small, so fragile, lying in his own refuse, his fur matted, his eyes dark as he glared up at me. There was so much distrust, so much pain, in his eyes, it made me want to reach out to him.

But I knew, especially in that moment, he was a wild animal, and I had to proceed with caution. So I opened his cage, sat back, and began to talk. I assured him he was safe, talking softly and with as much warmth and compassion as I could muster past the ache in my gut when he continued to glare at me uncomprehendingly.

When he first began to understand, I saw it in his eyes. And then his eventual surrender to my hands, to free him of those damn chains, was like a balm on my soul. My hands had been shaking with my frustration, and my blood had been chilled with my rage. But all of it calmed when he pressed his body beneath my hands.

But now, he might run. And though I would let him go, I wouldn't chase after him, I prayed to any gods listening that he wouldn't try. Because I had seen the cuts on his back and thighs from some kind of whip, and the festering wounds from the spiked collar around his neck would take his life in a matter of days if not treated.

I could only pray he would trust me, if only for long enough to get him back to some semblance of health.

I could see when he made his decision, those expressive eyes darkening with despair, and fear, but also a bit of hope. He shuffled forward, limping slightly, his tail between his legs, until he paused just a few feet in front of me. He tilted his head to the side and up, exposing his neck, and whined.

He was submitting to me.

I had seen the behavior in the keep's hounds, when they were training with the houndmaster, and I recognized the submissive gesture for what it was.

He was trusting me.

"That's it," I murmured, standing slowly so I didn't spook him. He watched me but didn't meet my eyes again. "Can you follow me, or do you need me to carry you?"

He was small for a wolf, but I figured he was still at least 60-70 pounds. I could carry him easily, but I wouldn't unless he gave me permission.

He chuffed in what I took as indignation, straightening and glaring up at me. I laughed and nodded in acquiescence.

"That's fine. Follow me, then."

I led him towards the gate, then turned left towards the keep's castle. The doctor's office and lab were on the main level so that it was easier to carry the injured to him. The little wolf followed at my feet, neither ahead of me nor behind me. His head was down, however, and his tail was still pressed up hard against his belly, his ears flat against his head.

"I don't know how much you can understand of what I'm saying, so I'm going to assume everything, and just hope I'm not talking to myself..." I began as we came up on the courtyard that led into the castle. The little wolf flinched back, lowering his body so that his belly was touching the ground, when we rounded on two guards who stood at attention when they saw me coming.

I put my finger to my lips, and Dasan and Nibley, two of my oldest and closest friends, froze, not calling out to greet me as they normally would. Luckily, most of the people in my keep were used to my idiosyncrasies, so they only shrugged, their eyes watching the wolf with amusement and curiosity as we passed them. I'd never hear the end of their questions and teasing once they found out about the wolf, but for now they let us pass in silence.

"The doctor's name is Gerard. He's a bit... gruff, but he's a good man. Once we get there, you'll probably want to... ah, change? Whatever it is you do to become a man. The doctor won't know the first thing about treating a wolf."

I could feel the wolf's eyes on me, but I kept my own ahead. We moved into the castle, and I turned down the east hall, towards the doctor's office. The wolf followed, his nose twitching as he began to falter. I could see his steps skipping, his limp more pronounced, and I paused, looking down at him. He was panting heavily now, and his eyes were glazing in pain.

"Please, little one," I pleaded, holding out a hand to him. "Let me help you. It's still a ways until we reach the doctor, and—"

I stopped as the wolf panted and then flopped down onto his belly, his legs curling up beneath him and his eyes watching me with an agony of emotions.

"I'm going to lift you up. I'm sorry if I hurt you. Please stay calm, alright?"

I leaned forward, putting one arm under his neck, the other under his rump, and lifted him to my chest. I simply held him for a moment, cataloging the way his entire body wracked with shivers, his warm breath on my arms, and the feel of his body wrapped up in mine.

And then he turned his head, looking up at me, and I almost fell to my knees.

Mine.

The thought was sudden and pervasive, and it hit me like an arrow out of nowhere, piercing my chest and making me flinch.

He watched me for a moment, and then he let his head drop onto my arm. His tongue lolled out as he continued to pant against me.

I shook myself, beginning the trek to the doctor's office again. I pushed the strange thoughts from my mind. I would examine them later, when I wasn't trying to save the life of an innocent... whatever he was.

The wolf's shaking began to quiet as I neared the office, and I hoped it was because he was warming up and calming, rather than what I feared: that he was losing consciousness.

I pushed the doctor's door open with my foot, laying the wolf on the nearest cot I could reach. He looked up at me, and though his eyes were glazed with fever and pain, he was fully conscious.

"I'll be right back. Can you try to... try to change? I'd like as few people as possible know about you... although the doc may be someone we need to tell. We'll see. Just... can you?"

The wolf huffed out a breath, and I took that as assent and ran to find the doctor the keep employed. He had a gruff exterior, but I knew he had a kind heart. He was one of about a dozen servants who had been in the keep since I was born. He had aided my mother during my birth.

When I dragged Gerard back to the cot, a dirty boy had taken the place of the wolf. He had pulled a blanket up over his groin, and he stared up at me and Gerard with barely-concealed panic.

"What is this?" Gerard muttered, yanking his hand out of my grip. I had woken him from bed, barely explaining anything other than that he was needed, but he had followed obediently.

Rather than waiting for an answer, Gerard moved towards the boy, reaching for his chin, presumably to lift it so he could inspect the abrasions on his neck. Luckily, he had fast reflexes, because just as he moved to grab the boy, the boy's teeth came down, snapping at the doctor just inches from his fingers.

He may have taken the fingers if the bite had landed.

"Fuck!" Gerard grunted, falling back just as I leapt forward.

"No!" I yelled, glaring the boy down. The boy stared up at me, confusion in his eyes, and chagrin. He bared his teeth, but I could see it was more out of fear than anger. "Stop it. He just wants to help."

"He almost bit me," Gerard hissed in disbelief, glaring the boy down. The boy's eyes widened as he met my eyes, and then he looked down, a blush rising to his pale cheeks. He dipped his head, as if in apology, and then tilted his head in submission.

"You're good now," I said to Gerard. "He was just startled. Come."

Gerard scoffed, muttering under his breath, and again reached towards the boy. He was more hesitant this time, but when Gerard reached the boy, I could see the heavy flinch the wolf boy couldn't hide.

I stayed nearby as Gerard told the boy to lie down, and then set to work. He cleaned a few of the wounds, his movements efficient but gentle, inspecting them, assessing them as he went. The boy stared up at the ceiling, reacting with a grimace only when the doctor prodded at a particularly deep wound. He seemed almost calm, content to lie and let the doctor do his job.

Until Gerard reached for the blanket covering his groin.

All became chaos as the boy roared furiously, sounding like a rage-filled war cry, jumping from the cot and landing in a crouch on the ground. He growled up at the doctor, and then turned eyes filled with betrayal on me.

And I knew in that instant, that if the man who had the boy imprisoned hadn't left town, I would find him, and I would rip his spine out through his fucking throat. Because that kind of reaction meant only one thing.

And I demanded satisfaction from the man who dared to touch what was mine that way.

Mine.

I pushed the cot out of the way, ignoring Gerard's hesitant confusion, and crouched near the boy.

"Kid, I need you to trust us. I know... I know you've been hurt, probably worse and in more ways than I dare to know. But we need your trust. We won't hurt you. And neither I, nor Gerard, would ever force ourselves on you. No one ever will again, so long as you are under my protection. Do you understand?"

I heard Gerard's soft intake of breath, and I knew he was beginning to understand the boy's reaction, as I had. The boy watched me, the betrayal dying in his eyes, replaced not by trust, but by a heady acceptance. He wasn't trusting that my words were true. He was giving himself up to me either way. Because he felt he had no choice.

Dammit. If it was the last thing I did, I would make sure he knew he was safe here. Safe with me.

He nodded, and then allowed me to help him back up onto the cot. His face flamed red as the doctor slowly pulled the sheet from his body and began to clean and inspect the wounds there. Once he had examined all of his wounds, Gerard turned to me.

"We have to get him clean. Then I can apply stitches to the wounds that need them, and bandages and ointment to the others. But until he's clean, I'm not comfortable closing up the wounds and surrounding them in bandages that will lock the filth in."

I could see the boy flinch, and I could almost feel his embarrassment.

"I'll be right back, kid, alright? I'm going to get you a bath ready."

The boy looked up at me, fear practically wafting off of him, but he nodded when I met his eyes with as much strength and truth in my eyes as I could. I tried to convey safety and warmth to him, because I knew so much of how animals communicated was through body language. And I hoped that something got through to him.

It took me only a moment to track down a servant in the hall and to order a hot bath brought to the doctor's office. And then I was rushing back to the boy. He was still lying on the cot, and when he saw me, his eyes lit up with relief.

And that should not have made pleasure dance down my spine. His trust was something I desperately wanted to earn, but it was not something that should affect me this much.

I moved to the boy, gently fingering one of his clenched fists. He stared up at me, his open expression shuttering as he stiffened at my touch. I lifted his hand into mine, carefully watching his reactions, and smiled when he didn't pull away from me.

I tried to think of all I knew about wolves, which wasn't much, I'll admit. And even if I knew more, I didn't know how much applied to this wolf, who wasn't quite a wolf; this boy who wasn't quite a boy.

I knew they were pack animals, so I figured touch, companionship, and just not being alone would be important for him. I highly doubted wolves in the wild spent much time, if any, alone. So hopefully my touch, as small as it was, would bring him comfort.

I also knew there were pack dynamics, alphas leading the packs, omegas being the lowest on the totem pole, so to speak. I wondered if that was something ingrained, or if it was taught. If this submissive wolf could learn to come out of his shell and stand up for himself. Or if he would always show his belly, tilt his neck towards me, ready for me to strike him, accepting that abuse was his lot in life.

When the servants were finished dumping hot water into the large tub and laying out soap and cloths, I helped the boy to his feet, lifting him easily in my arms when he faltered. He gasped but made no move to escape my arms. The sheet was back around his waist, and I held it in place when I lifted him. I let him down near the tub and held out my arm so he could hold it as he lowered himself into the water. He looked up at me, assessing, before dropping the sheet from around his waist to the ground and falling into the tub. I smiled at his haste and lifted the sheet up onto the nearest cot.

I kept my eyes down as I handed him one of the bars of medicinal soap and one of the cloths. And then I grabbed another, dipped it into the water, and flinched when I studied his back. There were whip marks, many that had healed badly, and fresh marks that looked like they were made with a heavy leather belt. There were long raised welts, ending in a deep, bruised cut— probably from the belt buckle.

"May I wash your back?" I asked gently, holding the cloth up and gesturing to him. He barely registered my words before he nodded, leaning forward, clutching the cloth and soap I had given him to his chest as if it were a lifeline.

I rubbed the soap into the cloth, lathering it up, and then knelt by the tub and gently stroked the cloth over his torn, bruised and scarred skin. For what felt like the hundredth time that day, I hoped the man who had kept this boy locked up was still nearby. I wanted to show him how it felt to have spikes dug into his neck and a belt buckle shoved up his ass.

I calmed myself, because I could feel the boy tensing beneath my hands, and breathed deeply through my nose.

"I'm sorry," I whispered once my breathing had cleared. The water was getting dirtied with dried and fresh blood as I tried to wash away everything that soiled him. "This... your treatment, it makes me angry. But it's not you, alright? I need you to know that you've done nothing wrong."

The boy jerked his shoulders in what I assumed was a shrug, and what I hoped was his acceptance of my words. I lathered up the cloth again, moving to the boy's shoulders, scrubbing as gently as I could when I reached the deep wounds on his neck.

I ended up helping him bathe completely. I had to call for the bath to be emptied and filled again before I helped him back in and ran the cloth and soap over him a last time. He let me move the cloth over his body, his eyes barely open as he stared dazedly ahead.

Washing his body should have been clinical— me helping a patient of Gerard's. A scared, injured young man. But as I reached his thighs, it became anything but. I fought back the heated thoughts that permeated through my mind, washing his limp cock and tight balls as quickly and efficiently as I could. I ignored the way they felt, heavy and warm and somehow right in my palm. I ignored the way he twitched and began to pant as my hand, covered in the soaped cloth, ran over his taint and anus. And I ignored the completely tense way he looked up at me, distrust and fear crossing his eyes before they shaded into a sort of calm acceptance.

The look I was really beginning to hate.

When I helped him from the bath, covering him in a towel, and led him back to Gerard, who waited with his ointments and tools ready, the boy was barely awake. He basically slept through Gerard's ministrations, and through it all, I kept my hold on his hand.

Because he had finally begun to grip me back.

5- A Lesson Easily Forgotten

✱ ****TRIGGER WARNING: Contains mentions of past rape and physical abuse.*****

EDON—

When I woke, it was to warmth. There was something heavy atop me, and my body was covered in something scratchy. But only over a few places. My wrists. My ankles, my neck, and a few spots on my back.

I lay for a moment, basking in the warmth, sure it was a dream. Master had never allowed me out of the cage, unless I was chained, and then only to his cart to service whomever had paid for me, but I knew I wasn't in the cage. For one, the wind wasn't beating at my thin skin. For another, there was silence all around. Silence, and warmth.

I took a deep breath, smelling only medicinal herbs, a fire that I could also now hear crackling, and female musk.

Just beside me.

I jerked up, staring down at a human female who lay curled up above the blankets that covered me.

The girl was a few years younger than me— maybe 12 or 13— with tightly curled hair so light it was nearly white, and soft gray eyes enhanced by dark black brows and lashes that watched me with surprise.

I yanked on the blankets, making sure they covered me, since I could feel that I was naked beneath them, and stared down at her in trepidation. Human females had never physically hurt me before, but they had never been kind, either.

"You're awake," she said unnecessarily. "Finally. You've been asleep for forever."

I looked around, testing the air and trying to scent anyone else. Someone had been in the room a few hours before, an older female, but her scent was almost completely faded. It was only me and this girl.

Why was she here?

The room I was in was large but cozy. Warm-colored rugs and tapestries covered the walls and floors, holding in the warmth that poured from the giant hearth on the other side of the room. The bed I lay on— I was on a bed! — had four thick blankets that covered me, as well as dozens of pillows I had been laying my head on.

As I stared around the room, my memories began to come back. Master's beating. The crowd. The man with the icy eyes. The doctor. The bath. Then... nothing.

Why was I here?

"Lhiam said to leave you alone, to let you rest. But I got bored, and I was curious. He's such a stick in the mud sometimes. He never lets me do anything I want to. You know it took him almost a week to bring me to the carnival? I had to wait around until that bitch from Kar'a left, and then..."

I watched the girl, almost amused at her chattering. She was cute, for a human, with little freckles across her cheeks and nose, and a full, pert mouth. I sat back against the pillows, unsure what else to do until the girl stopped talking, or something else happened.

"Oh, look at me, talking away, when you must be starving!" she finally said, and my ears perked up at that. I held a hand to my stomach, which chose that moment to growl. She let out a laugh and looked at me apologetically. "Of course you are. Like I said, you've been asleep for two days. Let me call someone for you. And I know my cousin will want to know you're awake."

I nodded as she paused, as if to ask my permission, and a wide smile broke across her face.

"See, you can understand me. Tate didn't believe Lhiam, but Lhiam was sure of it. I'm glad. You seem very sweet. It would be a shame if you were stupid."

I held back a laugh, and then sniffed the air again as a new scent hit my nose. I was jerked out of my bemusement by the scent of a male approaching. I scented him, but he wasn't familiar. Which meant he wasn't the man with the icy eyes, and he wasn't the doctor— Gerard.

Had the man with the ice eyes lied to me? Had he only gotten me clean and dressed my wounds for a new master?

I would never acknowledge the small wedge of pain in my gut at the thought. Gods, I had believed him. If only for a moment, I had felt safe in his arms. His touch had been like a balm. After being neglected for so long, only being touched when it was to inflict pain, he had kept his hands on me only to offer comfort.

But it had been a lie.

He had sold me. Left me with another man. Left me alone again.

I would be used again. Dirty again. He would touch me. Put his hands—

My thoughts were broken when the man kicked the large door open, fury engulfing the room in the waves wafting from him. I recognized him as the man who had taken me from Master, the one who had driven me to wherever I had been with the man with icy eyes.

The man who smelled of fire.

He froze when he spotted me on the bed, his eyes roaming from me to the girl at my side and back again. And then his eyes shuttered dangerously, and I smelled the blood lust that rolled off of him.

Directed at me.

I knew instinctively that he wouldn't hurt the girl, especially since I smelled no fear from her. Only chagrin, and a bit of annoyance. But the fear that ripped through my body was heady, and overwhelming. It took over, forcing me to leap back, my nakedness forgotten as I backed into the corner of the bed and the wall, curling into a ball, as small as I could make myself. I made sure my stomach, and thus most of my vital organs, was covered, my entire body shaking so violently I could hear my teeth chatter.

Images flashed through my mind so quickly, I was left dizzy. Master's belt on my back. His booted feet against my ribs. Coughing up blood as he laughed, then dragged me by my hair into the cart for the group of men who waited for me.

The men who had paid to fuck a monster.

The man seemed shocked for a moment, but then he held his hand out to the girl, who stared at me as if I had smacked her, and called out to her.

"Lacy, come here. Slowly."

"Tate, he's not—"

"Now, Lacy," the man hissed, one hand outstretched to her, the other clenched into a fist at his side. I stared at that fist as if my life depended on watching it.

Because it likely did.

The girl stood with a huff of irritation, turning her back to me and sauntering over to the man. When she reached his side, he gripped her arm so tightly I could see white finger indents in her arm.

I growled, my fury superseding my terror. But only for a moment, because then his eyes were back on me, the girl was shoved behind him, and I couldn't breathe for the terror that was rolling through my body. He took a step forward, towards me, and I choked, gasping as I held my hands up, trying to hold him back.

I knew it would be useless. It always was. He would hurt me. He would make me bleed. He would rip me open and leave me in the darkness. And there was nothing I could do about it. No crying or pleading would do me any good.

I learned that very quickly with my first master.

It was not a lesson easily forgotten.

The man froze again, his eyes assessing me. The fury I could still smell had lessened to a degree, but it was still a heady thing that I wanted to reach out and shove away.

"Tate, listen to me," the girl, Lacy, complained from behind the man. "He wasn't gonna hurt me. Lhiam—"

"Your cousin told you to stay away from this room, Princess!" the man yelled, and I had to fight back the growl that rolled to my throat. Why did I think I could protect the girl, when I couldn't even protect myself?

"Tate!" a voice called from outside the door. A voice I recognized. A voice that sent a chill of pleasure down my spine, and made my entire body begin to relax as a warmth of calm came over me.

I stiffened as he came through the door, refusing to let myself fall into the man's trap. He looked from me to the other man— Tate— then to Lacy, then back to me again. His face fell as he studied me, and he held his hands out imploringly. Pleadingly.

"What's wrong, kid?" he murmured, his voice soft, soothing.

Liar! I wanted to shout at him. But I couldn't. Even if I remembered how to speak, my throat was closed with fear, and my breaths were coming too fast.

"What happened?" he asked, directing his words to Lacy and Tate when I refused to budge. I only backed myself further into the wall, looking around for a way to escape. The bandages on my wrists, ankles and neck hid the mostly-healed wounds, and I thought I might have the strength to run if I could just get past the men.

But if they caught me, I knew I couldn't fight. I was weak from hunger, and from thirst and blood loss. I would be a pathetic opponent if they managed to catch me.

"Tate scared him!" Lacy yelled, her little lips pursing out into a pout. I was momentarily frozen as I stared down at her. Because she had moved out from behind Tate and was stepping towards me again.

Tate grabbed her arm again, yanking her back, and I leapt to the edge of the bed, keeping myself crouched to try to protect my softest parts. I growled at the man as he tried to pull the struggling girl behind him, and all three humans froze.

Let her go! I wanted to scream. Instead, I growled again, glaring into the man's eyes and baring my teeth. I let the shift begin to come over me, so my fangs sharpened, and the girl gasped.

"Calm down, everyone!" the man with icy eyes muttered in annoyance, stepping towards me and then turning back to glare at the man and girl behind him. Putting his back to me. "Both of you, out! He's been through enough!"

"But Lhiam—" the girl began, just as Tate said, "Your highness—"

The man cut both off. "Get out. Now."

With the man's words, obedience was quick. I worried for the girl for a moment, until the man turned to me, after shutting the door behind him, and smiled gently.

"She'll be fine. He won't hurt her. He was only worried about her."

6- Misunderstanding

L HIAM

I had never wanted to punch Tate more than I did as I walked into the guest chambers and caught sight of the wolf boy crouching in the corner, so terrified he was hyperventilating. I promised the boy he was safe here, and no sooner was he awake than someone was threatening him.

I was shocked at the boy's reaction to Tate grabbing Lacy. I knew the guard was only worried about her safety— he didn't trust the boy— but the boy didn't seem to think the same way. He leapt forward, growling, his teeth elongating and sharpening as we all stared in shock.

I could almost see what had happened. Lacy, in all her precocious, adventurous glory, had probably gone into the boy's room, woken him, and then talked his ear off. Tate, hearing from her maids or tutors that she had escaped them again, had probably spent most of his morning looking for her, before realizing where she was.

And despite my words of trust for the wolf boy, Tate had automatically assumed the worst. He was a wild animal, a male, left alone with an all-but-defenseless girl.

But if harming her had ever crossed the boy's mind, he didn't show it. He merely glared at me as I shoved both Lacy and Tate out the door, and then turned back to him.

"I promise, that was a misunderstanding. You're still safe here. Please, don't be afraid. We won't hurt you."

The boy scoffed, the voice sounding more human than wolf for the first time since I'd found him, and shuffled back. He grabbed one of the smaller blankets, pulling it over his shoulders as he continued to shake.

"I know you don't believe me right now, but you'll see. I'll earn your trust."

The boy met my eyes again, then gestured to the door behind me. I understood immediately.

"Like I told you before, you can leave anytime," I began, and watched in frustration as the boy almost tripped over himself as he pushed to his feet. "But," I finished, holding my hand up to stop him. "You have a warm bed, and food here. Please, at least eat before you go. We've been waking you to feed you broth, but you were never awake long, and it wasn't enough. If you can get it down, you need real food."

The boy's nod was reluctant, but when it finally came I smiled. I would take his acceptance as a victory, small as it was.

I left for a moment, in search of a servant to bring the boy something to eat, and when I returned, he was by the large window, staring out into the forest behind the keep. I could tell he knew I was there, because his ears burned red and his body tensed as I entered the room. I sat on one of the large armchairs near the fire, hoping he would soon feel comfortable enough to join me. I could see his shoulders shaking slightly, and I knew that the fever he had fought off for the last two days had finally broken, leaving him weak and most likely freezing with lack of sustenance.

"I would like to ask you a few questions, if you would feel comfortable enough for that," I began, keeping my voice low. "You don't have to answer them, but I must admit to some curiosity over you. Once I know a bit more, we can figure out what to do next, as well."

The wolf boy finally looked away from the window, turning to face me. He met my eyes, but his gave little away. For the first time, his eyes were shuttered of any emotion.

The arrival of the servant bearing a tray of broth, meats, cheeses, and tea made him tense and I could see him baring his teeth at the maid, but she paid him little attention. She merely set the tray on the table by the fire, bowed to me, and exited.

I waved my hand at the food. "Please, eat, kid. You need to get your strength up."

The boy— gods I needed to find out his name, because calling him boy was just sad— moved hesitantly to the tray, his eyes never leaving mine. When he reached the tray, he lowered himself to the ground and began to dig in ravenously. I held back my frustration that he had sat on the ground rather than the perfectly comfortable armchair near the table.

"What's your name?" I asked, once he had managed to pack away most of the food and he seemed to be slowing in his eating. He froze and glanced up at me before shrugging.

"Does that mean you don't know, or that you don't care what I call you?" I asked, trying to calm my annoyance. I wanted his trust; I wanted to know everything about him. And he was not cooperating with me at all.

The boy turned fully to me, clutching at his blanket and tilting his head up at me. Not in submission, but in question.

And I finally understood.

"You can't speak...?"

The boy motioned at his neck, flinching when his fingers came in contact with the bandage there. He shrugged and shook his head.

"Alright, that's fine. We can figure out another way to communicate. I know one of the maids here has a sister who can't speak, and they use some sort of hand signals to talk to her. We can ask her to show us those, if you'd like. For now, though, I'd like to figure out a name for you. I'd like to stop thinking of you as 'boy.'"

The boy's eyes widened with indignation and I could almost see the words in his mind.

I'm not a child.

I chuckled, which seemed to only anger him more, which then amused me further. He growled, the sound coming from deep in his chest, as he glared me down.

"Sorry, sorry," I mumbled, rubbing at my mouth to wipe the smile that still lingered there away. "So, a name. We could go with something classic. Like Michael. George. Henry."

The boy's nose wrinkled and he pointed at me. I froze, shame rushing through me. "I never introduced myself?" The boy shook his head and I sighed. "My apologies. That was rude of me, although under the circumstances, I think you can maybe find it in your heart to forgive me. I am Lhiam."

The boy nodded, as if in greeting, and I smiled. "So, Henry. That was my father's name. Do you like it?"

He shook his head, his nose wrinkling again. "This would be much easier if you held up hands to show how much you hate the name. Five fingers for hating it a lot, one finger if you like it. So on that scale, how much do you hate the name Hen—"

"— Edon," the wolf boy mumbled, his eyes meeting mine with determination. His voice was raspy, gravelly, like a rock slide, but it was clear as music.

"Edon," I repeated, unsure how to move forward, or even breathe, with the object that had seemed to lodge itself in my throat. "Your name is Edon?"

Edon nodded, then ducked his head.

"Haven't... spoken. Long time," he murmured, the sound still quiet, unsure. "Wasn't sure... still could."

A stabbing pain dug its way into my chest as I nodded down at him, smiling in a way I hoped was reassuring.

"Were you with that...man for long?" I asked, wanting to call that monster anything but a man. He was less than a man. He was less than an animal. He was a monster, a disgusting breed of human filth.

Edon shrugged, his eyes shuttering. This time with pain, rather than lack of emotion.

"You don't know how long?"

He shook his head in agreement.

"Do you have family you can go back to? Did he take you from family?"

Edon shook his head again, and I couldn't help the stab of agony I felt in my gut when I saw the pain in his eyes. The grief.

I wanted nothing more than to reach forward and grab the small man into my arms. To comfort him, to bring warmth to his freezing limbs, and to never let go. But I knew my touch would be unwelcome. I knew he needed space.

So I would give it to him.

No matter how much it cost me to hold myself back.

7- Awake and Hungry

E DON

    After reassuring me that I could stay as long as I needed, and he would find a job for me if I wanted to continue to stay after I was healed, Lhiam left me to rest. It was only once he was gone that I noticed the pair of clothes that hung on a wardrobe on the other side of the room from the fire. I quickly dressed in the loose shirt, undergarments and cotton leggings, before falling back into the warm bed.

I was woken what felt like moments later, but I knew must have been hours. The light outside the window was different, and I could see that the sun was about to set. The doctor, Gerard, was leaning over me, his fingers lightly fingering my injuries. He was muttering, seeming almost distressed, or confused, but another voice, one that had me pressing myself away from the doctor to be closer to that voice, quieted him, calmed him.

I whined deep in my throat, but Lhiam's hands clutching mine calmed me instantly and I felt myself falling back under.

The next time I woke, I was alone. The fire was still high in the hearth, but the chill that had pervaded my bones for as long as I could remember was gone. I was warm, inside and out. I pulled myself from the bed, scenting the air. It was just after sunrise, and I could smell the morning dew evaporating in the weak autumn sun.

The bandages on my body were gone, leaving behind scars and a few bruises and raised welts that were healing a bit slower than they should.

I jumped from the bed, shifting in midair and landing in my wolf form. I stretched, reveling in the feeling of my muscles crying out at the unfamiliar freedom I had. I wanted more than anything to run. To find my way into the woods, to simply run, and to never stop.

But Lhiam's face flashed in my mind, pleading with me to give him a chance to prove himself trustworthy. His voice soothing me. His hands on mine warm, kind, and gentle. And I knew I would stay. I couldn't leave, because something about him drew me in.

And I could only hope that wouldn't be the end of me.

I was jerked out of my thoughts by a frustrated scream. I recognized the voice immediately— it was Lacy. I could hear no fear in her voice, nor smell it in the air, but she was annoyed, and she was angry.

I scratched at the cracked-open door with my paws until it swung open, and was immediately met with a sight that had my hackles raised and a growl rising in my chest.

Lacy was backed against the wall, her face red with barely suppressed fury. A man, at least three times her age and size, hung over her, leering down at her.

He was in the middle of a sentence, but my growl cut him off and he jumped and turned.

"Fucking hell," he muttered as he began to back away. I saw Lacy's amusement as she positioned herself behind me. I began to move towards the man, bearing my teeth and putting as much menace behind my growl as I possibly could. Before long, he turned and ran, looking back a few times to ensure I wasn't following him.

When I was sure he wasn't coming back, I turned back to Lacy and whined gently.

"I'm fine, Edon," she answered my unspoken question. "Thanks for that. He's one of Lhiam's councilors, and he keeps trying to get me to..." She trailed off, shaking her head. "Well, let's just say they're all a bunch of power-hungry assholes and leave it at that."

I chuffed in amusement just as my stomach growled loudly, the sound echoing off the stone halls around us. Lacy smiled and then laughed.

"I came to see if you were awake and hungry. I guess you've now answered both questions. C'mon, I have a breakfast ready for us."

I followed the young girl with an almost bemused sort of acceptance. I had never met someone like her before. She spoke to me as if there was nothing strange about me being a man who could turn into a wolf (or a wolf to a man— I was never really sure which I was), as if we had known each other for years, and were dear friends. Something about that attitude had me following like a pup follows the alpha female.

8- Guard and Companion

✷ ***Some fun, imagined smut ahead...** ****

LHIAM

For days now, my thoughts had been on nothing but Edon. Both Stefan and Tate had yelled at me for my lack of attention in meetings and other activities, and just that morning Tate had managed to throw me on my ass five times while we trained together. But I couldn't seem to bring myself to care. Because everything I was was directed to that small guest room, where the little wolf man was sleeping.

A few hours after our conversation, I had accompanied the doctor to change Edon's bandages. I had held onto his hands, as he had seemed to seek out comfort, but when the doctor removed the bandages, the injuries were all but healed. Only a few raised, sore-looking scars and bruises remained to show the torture the wolf man had been through.

Gerard had been upset, confused, and annoyed at the rapidly healing wounds. I had been forced to tell him about Edon— all I knew, at least. That he wasn't quite human, although I wasn't sure what that made him. Once I was finished, he had calmly removed the bandages and nodded after each was removed. We had both simply had to accept that there would be things about Edon we might not really understand.

Like how he had healed in days rather than weeks.

My thoughts drifted again to that beautiful body of his. His thin, pale face; those huge, expressive eyes. And those lips that had my cock twitching with interest as I pictured pressing my own lips to them, my tongue seeking to mate with his as our bodies pressed tightly against each other. His gasp of breath as I took his hard cock in hand, using his own wetness to ease my way. Pressing my fingers against the head as I swallowed his moans, tasting each one. I would gently make my way down his squirming body, trying to keep calm as his whimpers turned into pleading. I would bring him to the edge, over and over, before calming, stilling, to drag him back down. When I finally penetrated him, joining our bodies as one, he would scream, howl to the ceiling as I swallowed down every cry he uttered. And when I finally let him come, I would hold myself back so I could watch him come apart in my arms— only to start all over again.

By the time I was finished with him, he wouldn't remember his own name, much less any that came before me. I would make sure he only saw me. Only tasted me.

I would be his last, and he would be mine.

Mine.

"Your Highness," Stefan all but snarled, his big belly shaking with his irritation. "Did you hear anything Louis just said?"

I shook my head, noticing that my body had reacted to my musings as I sat and listened to Louis whine about something. Louis was one of my twelve councilors— one of the youngest at 37, and also the only one as yet unwed. His voice was high and nasally, and his hair was greasy and slicked back heavily against his head.

"I wasn't listening. Please, can you repeat what you said?"

Louis seemed taken aback by my rudeness, but Stefan simply sighed.

"That wolf you brought in, for some gods-forsaken reason I still cannot comprehend, attacked him and the princess this morning," Stefan articulated, speaking clearly as if to a small child. "I warned you that wild animals do not make good pets, and this is the proof. I would ask that you— "

"Where is my cousin?" I asked, cutting off Stefan's words. The man could drone on for hours if left speaking.

"She's having brunch in the south garden," Tate answered. I looked over at him, and saw the amusement in his eyes, so I knew she was safe.

"I'll speak with her, and I'll resolve the issue. If you were injured, you should see Gerard, Louis."

Louis mumbled something, but I ignored him. I had been in the council room for hours, and my head was bursting to escape. I excused myself for lunch and made my way to the south garden. On the way, I could hear a few whispers about wild animals being let in the castle, and a few about Lacy. She had always been a bit of an oddball, and I had allowed her oddities, even encouraged them, because they reminded me so much of her mother, my cousin. But I knew that the things I allowed her made her different in the eyes of many people. She was not a docile, quiet, genteel lady. She was loud, and she was precocious, and she was brave.

And I loved her all the more for it.

When I made my way through the small gate into the south garden, I froze at the sight before me. Lacy sat on one of the benches near the pond in the middle of the garden, with Edon in his wolf form panting lightly at her feet. She read aloud from a thick tome of fairy tales I recognized as one that had belonged to her mother when we were children together. A finished meal sat on the bench next to her, and I was grateful that Edon seemed to have shared her meal, since I could see two sets of plates.

Edon noticed me first, if his body stiffening and his growl was any indication. But when he caught sight of me, he jerked his head back. His ears flattened against his head, and he whined, lowering his head and tilting his neck in submission.

Dammit. He had looked so calm and content before he had seen me.

Lacy looked up from her book and smiled at me with that gentle, joyful smile she only seemed to ever grace me with.

"Lhiam!" she said softly, her eyes flicking to the wolf, as if afraid to spook him. "Sorry, but we've already finished lunch, cousin."

I nodded, making my way to the bench Lacy leaned her back against. I ran a hand through my hair when the wolf belly-crawled over to Lacy, putting his head on her lap and refusing to look at me. She seemed taken aback, but she gently set her hand on the wolf's head and looked up at me, concern marking each of her features.

"Thanks, Lacy. I'll have lunch back in my study. I wanted to speak with Edon about something." I paused, looking down at the wolf, whose eyes were wide with awareness and whose ears twitched as he felt my gaze on him. "I've heard you accosted one of my councilors."

I said the words almost in jest, to see what kind of reaction I could get out of the wolf, but the one I got had my heart rending in two. The wolf jerked back, showing his teeth, putting distance between himself and Lacy, and then cowering. Expecting a blow, and making sure Lacy wasn't caught in the crossfire.

Lacy gasped and glared up at me. "He did no such thing. Louis was—"

I smiled and held up a hand, effectively cutting Lacy off. "I'm aware of Louis' proclivities, and it worries me that he has confronted you again... I'd like to ask a favor of you, Edon. I want to offer you a job. One, I think, only you can do."

Edon stood a little straighter, maybe knowing now that the blow he had expected wouldn't be coming, but he still refused to meet my eyes, and his posture remained the same: cowering, submissive. Defeated.

"A guard and companion for Lacy is needed; one who can follow her, keep up with her, and yet let her keep the freedom I know she desires above all else. You would basically be her companion, and I believe, for the most part, your presence alone would deter many... unsavory characters, like Louis."

The wolf finally met my eyes, and I saw the question there. The hesitation.

"Lacy is my cousin, but she is more like my daughter." Lacy scoffed, rolling her eyes, but I could see her cheeks pink with warmth at my words. I knew she felt the same way for me as I did for her. "Her safety is second to nothing to me. There would be many times where there would be other guards to assist you, but I know my cousin gets into mischief when none know she is even missing. I would expect you to assert any amount of force to keep her safe and comfortable."

The wolf cocked his head, studying me and then finally pulling himself up straight and meeting my eyes wholly— not in submission, but in answer.

"You will be paid for your time, and room and board are, of course, included. You will be safe, little wolf," I finished, hoping he heard the sincerity in my words.

Finally, after watching me for a few minutes, the wolf nodded and moved to sit beside Lacy again.

Lacy squealed in excitement, and I saw the wolf's amusement and affection as he looked up at Lacy. I was surprised the girl had stayed silent so long while I offered the job to Edon.

"I'm so excited!" she tittered, wrapping her arms around the wolf and digging her face into his neck. I could see the poor male stiffen, obviously uncomfortable with the show of affection, before he softened and nuzzled her thick head of hair. "We're going to have such fun!"

I snuck out of the garden, smiling at the wolf's amusement at the girl's antics, and passed a frowning Tate. I shook my head at him, refusing to argue with him, and jerked my head back at the princess and wolf that were again in their own world.

"Set up a monthly stipend. Get him clothes and a room near Lacy— there is an empty one right next door to hers, if I remember correctly."

I moved past Tate before I could even see his nod of obedience, and as I walked away, I could feel Edon's eyes on my back. Studying me. Watching me.

For nearly two weeks, I watched from afar as Edon made himself at home. I could see him gradually relaxing, and I knew Lacy was a large part of that. She dragged him around on her various adventures and he followed, usually in his wolf form. But occasionally I would be graced with his human form. And those times were seared in my mind for hours after. I couldn't even count how many times I was forced to seek out solitude as thoughts of him completely took over me. But I kept my distance, because I knew he needed time. And I didn't know how much control I would have over myself if I was left alone with him again.

I heard the stories of the princess's new pet, however. Many were amused, many had grown to love the small wolf. But others were angry, and fearful.

Stefan and Louis still had a grudge against the wolf, but from what Lacy told me, that was only because Louis couldn't even get near her without being chased off by Edon. Tate was more relaxed than he had ever been. With the wolf by her side almost 24 hours a day, except when she slept, she was safer than she'd ever been.

And with time, Tate's trust was beginning to be earned. He began to see the same things I saw: the softness in Edon's eyes as he watched Lacy, the protectiveness whenever anyone came near, and the way his eyes and body were always alert. He took his job seriously, and he protected her with everything he had.

Every once in awhile, Edon would choose to follow Lacy in his human form. She treated him much the same way, no matter what his form, and he watched her with his amused affection no matter if he had fur or not. I made sure the man was outfitted properly— with cotton shirts, leather tunics, and breeches and leggings. I had Tate give him a dagger, and I could see it hanging from his hip while he escorted Lacy to the library one morning, but I knew it would likely never be used. If Edon had to use violence to protect Lacy, his opponent would be brought down by tooth and claw, not a silver dagger.

I very rarely heard him speaking, and he was known in the castle as a silent man. The only time he ever really spoke, unless he was answering a direct query, was when he was with Lacy. I even saw him smiling a bit at her a few times as she laughed at something he had said.

Knowing we needed an identity for the man, I had Tate tell him to say he was a distant cousin of Tate's, come to the castle to train as a guard. To perpetuate this, and to Tate's insistence, Tate began to train Edon every morning while Lacy was with her tutors. For a few hours, Tate showed Edon how to fight hand-to-hand. He skipped over weapons-training, saying the wolf would be a better fighter if he wasn't hampered by weaponry, and I had to agree. Watching him jumping lithely around Tate, eluding the bigger man with a graceful ease, shifting back and forth from man to wolf, it was like a dance the wolf man was mastering before my eyes.

I encountered him only a half dozen times in those first few days. Each time, he stiffened, bowed, and then seemed to stand awkwardly, at a loss for what to do next. I stayed at a distance, watching him come into his own, but I could see he wasn't fully himself yet, wasn't quite comfortable where he was, so I continued to stay away. I would smile politely at him, nod, and then escape as quickly as possible. Because I feared if I stayed longer, I would do something to frighten him away, to make him bolt. And that I would then spend the rest of my life kicking myself for pushing away what I feared, and hoped, was the other half of my soul.

He was just learning to live outside of a cage. He didn't need a love-struck, much older man dragging him down while he was just learning to fly.

9- At Home

EDON

The first few weeks in the castle went by in a blur. Each morning, I convinced myself to stay one more day. Each night, I called myself a liar and admitted I had no plans to leave.

I had never felt so much at home. Not since I was a child in Ma and Pa's cottage.

It was a feeling I relished, and one I attributed to one man. One man who had been steadily ignoring me since he asked me to stay and gave me a job. One man who wouldn't leave my mind, no matter how I tried to distract myself.

He was truly a beautiful male, if that word could be attributed to a man. His hair was blonde, but with touches of red when the light shone on it right. His jaw was strong, and he was almost always perfectly clean-shaven.

But every once in awhile, when I could sense he'd had a long day, or hadn't slept well the night before, a slight smattering of stubble would be drawn across his skin, accentuating the lines of his jaw and the smoothness of his lips. He had full, pale lips that drew me in every time he spoke. Almost like he was purposely pursing them and licking them as he spoke just to draw my eyes.

I had never felt so attracted to someone— had never really been attracted to anyone at all, really. It was like a physical pull, like he had a rope attached to my chest, drawing me in.

But ever since I woke, ever since I was able to eat on my own, and began to heal, he had treated me like a pariah. I approached him a few times, not quite sure what I wanted, what I would say. But just wanting to be near him; craving the sound of his voice. But each time he answered for me, because he would act politely, sometimes even say a few words of greeting, ask how I was, before disappearing. Before running away.

Because I may be completely clueless when it came to human social constructs, but even I couldn't mistake a man running from something. Or someone.

I spent my days with Lacy, and then with Tate. Lacy dragged me into town on multiple occasions, spending her days among the people in the little town below the keep. She helped a hedge witch pick herbs and weed her garden, aided a hunter in skinning his latest catch, and spent days watching the town blacksmith forge weapons. She barely seemed to notice the sweat dripping down her skin as she sat far too close to the fire, listening intently as the blacksmith explained each step he took. She had excitedly told me that he had promised he would help her make her own dagger for her sixteenth birthday, and so until then she was studying with him.

She seemed to have a fascination with the goings-on in the town, and in the castle. She helped the head chef put together breakfast, waking before the sun rose. I followed her and slept near the fireplace in the kitchen. The head chef seemed to have a certain sort of gruff affection for me, despite his initial protestations that dogs didn't belong in the kitchen, because on the second day I was there, a plate of marrow rich bones sat waiting for me by the fire. My room, a small, cozy, warm space, was just beside Lacy's, so I always knew when she was sneaking in or out and I was able to follow her silently, no matter the time of day or night.

Her excitement, her genuine care for the simple day-to-day of the people around her, and her pure affection she bestowed on everyone she saw, made her universally beloved. But there were a few eyes, many older men and some women who wore rich silks and furs, who showed their distaste. They watched her, and me, like we were some dirty question they couldn't find the answer to. That they wanted to be rid of. But Lacy ignored them, so I did too. I stayed near her, and I watched her, and I kept silent.

It wasn't that she couldn't see them. She knew they were there, she noticed them, but she kept her thoughts, her frustrations to herself. It showed a strength that made me proud of my little mistress.

On the second or third morning after I had woken, while Lacy was sequestered in the library with her various tutors, I was dragged into a sort of training yard by Tate. I had been waiting outside the library in my human form, ready to spend the next few hours sleeping, waiting for Lacy, when Tate demanded I follow him. I followed reluctantly, never really comfortable with the man who had so frightened me when I first woke in this strange, new place.

The big man had barely said a word before he attacked me. I jumped back, out of his range, watching him in confusion. There was no rage, no blood-lust, and no fear coming from the man. Only a sort of patient determination. So why was he attacking me?

"If you're going to be protecting the princess, you need to know how to do more than bite and claw."

And with that, our training sessions began. Tate did seem to understand that any time I fought, it would likely be without the aid of any kind of weaponry, and for that I was grateful. If I only learned how to fight with a sword, and I had to shift in the middle of a battle, I would lose the only advantage I had.

I was never fully comfortable with Tate. Even after half a dozen training sessions with him, I still never left him at my back, and I kept one eye on him whenever he was near. He was a dangerous man, and I needed to keep that in mind. He didn't seem to mind my caution, as he basically ignored me except during our hours of training. Every day, just before I left the training yard, he would remind me to eat more. That I needed to bulk up, if I was ever going to fight more than children and women with my stature.

And each day I shook my head in annoyance. The constant reminders that I was too skinny, too small, were everywhere. With the three meals a day I was getting being near the princess, I had definitely gained weight. I could no longer count each of my ribs, my skin had a sort of healthy glow I had never seen on myself before, and the gauntness of my cheeks and purple under my eyes was greatly reduced. But I would never be a large male. I was the size of a woman, barely much bigger than Lacy, and I knew that nothing I ate, or did, would change that.

My years with my masters had taken their toll, and my body reminded me of that with each morning that I woke in a sweat of nightmares, if I slept at all, my scars stretching across my back and shoulders. Most nights I didn't sleep. I roamed the halls in my wolf form. In this way, I had made a sort of silent friendship with a few of the night guards, who seemed happy with my company as they watched over the soundless castle as the moon shone above us. Two in particular— a large man named Nibley and another, shorter but no less muscular male named Dasan, seemed to take an instant liking to me. I never saw them in the daytime, but when I wandered the halls in my wolf form, I sometimes found them and joined them in their vigil. After the first day, Nibley even began to bring me hunks of meat and bones with the marrow still fresh inside.

It took me two of these nights to first notice that they were more to each other than simply work partners. I had just come around a corner when I caught the scent of aroused male, pre-cum, and sweat. I froze, the smells hitting me like a jackhammer to my fear. It was a familiar scent, and not one I associated with pleasantly. Memories of my past had already driven me from my bed, and now I was confronted with the scent that plagued so many of my horrible nightmares.

But then the sounds hit me and I jerked forward, toward the writhing bodies, almost against my will. There were soft, gentle whispers, gasps of pleasure, and low moans that hit me low in the belly, drawing a sort of heat through my body as I imagined the sounds coming from Lhiam. I had no idea why his face popped into my mind, but when it did, the heat that pressed itself down my spine intensified.

As I drew near, I could make out, by the light of the moon through the slated windows, Nibley pressing Dasan up against the wall, mostly hidden from view by a tapestry that covered the alcove they occupied. Both men had their breeches down around their ankles, and one of Dasan's legs was wrapped around Nibley's hips, his other foot standing on tiptoe to thrust up against the taller man crowding him against the wall. I could see flashes of their hard, erect cocks pressing against each other and against each other's hard abdomens, slicked by pre-cum and spit. Both of them still had their shirts on their shoulders, but they were completely unbuttoned, their skin rubbing against the other's.

"Harder, Nib," Dasan whimpered, his head shooting back as he moaned. "I'm so close, husband."

I watched in fascination as Nibley's ass cheeks clenched as he thrust erratically against Dasan, mouthing and tonguing at his exposed neck as he gasped against the other man.

"So good for me, my love," Nibley whispered against the other man's throat, and with his words Dasan stiffened and then seemed to melt against Nibley. "Come, love. Come for me."

The scent of pre-cum heightened as Dasan bit down on Nibley's shoulder, his eyes flashing with ecstasy as his body began to spasm, his leg around Nibley tightening. Then the scent of cum hit me like a rabid bear, and I jerked back, huffing in fear. But I didn't want to leave my new friends. There was something so... right about what I had seen. Something inside of me told me that this was right, and everything I had ever experienced was a perversion of this loving act between these two men.

Dasan's eyes met mine from around Nibley's gasping, jerking form, and Dasan grunted in amusement.

"We have a voyeur, my love."

Nibley turned quickly, and when his eyes fell on me, his own amusement was clear. "Gods but if he isn't the most intelligent mutt I've ever seen. Look at how he's watching us. Like he knows... I don't know, things."

Dasan chuckled and shook his head. He reached down, running a hand up his abdomen, scooping up the thin streams of cum from his stomach, and then began to lick his fingers. I chuffed, fascinated by the pleasure in his eyes as he licked up his and Nibley's release. Master had liked for me to eat his cum, as had a few of the men my second Master had sold me to, but it had never been a pleasurable experience for me. It had always been forced down my throat by dirty fingers, or even worse, dirty cocks.

I couldn't count how many times I had spewed vomit all over the men when they tried to force their cum down my throat. And the beatings I got afterwards, for not pleasing the men, were always brutal to a new extreme. Those were the times when my Master got extra creative in his torments.

"We should get back to work," Nibley whispered as he helped Dasan put his pants back on and then began to button his own shirt. "Captain said we had 30 minutes for break... I think it's been longer than that."

"It has most definitely been longer than that, husband," Dasan laughed, quirking a brow and looking Nibley up and down. "I could never only have you for 30 minutes."

Nibley blushed— and if that wasn't a strange sight, an almost-40-year-old man blushing, I didn't know what was.

Once they were dressed, I followed the men to their post, just outside the southern wall, and watched them for the rest of the night. Nibley spoke to me a few times, nonsense like people always speak to animals, but otherwise they seemed to be content to stand with me, and with each other, in silence.

I'd admit, I had never seen two men together in the way they had been. Hadn't even heard of it. The only experience I had with that was my own nightmares, my forced nights underneath various men who laughed at my blood and my pain. But neither Nibley nor Dasan had seemed reluctant; both had been wholly excited by the other. And I could see, even in my confused state, that it was more than physical between the big, older men. There had been affection, love, like I had seen between my ma and pa when I was a pup. There had been genuine caring as Dasan licked up their joined release, and as Nibley helped Dasan to dress. The whispered words of love, the gasps of pleasure— that was nothing like I had ever seen before. Ever felt before.

And it left a longing in me I had never felt before. Because as I continued to watch them through the night, I noticed for the first time the gentle touches as Dasan handed Nibley the skein of water they kept near them through their vigil. The soft, whispered sighs when their eyes met, and the way the very air between them seemed to be rife with a sort of tightness, almost as if there was nothing between them. As if, no matter how far apart they stood, they were joined.

And as these thoughts raced through my mind, I felt that longing deepen, along with the reappearance of Lhiam's eyes. His lips. His tongue dipping into my mouth as he owned me. My own cries in his ears as he grunted in mine, his hot breath against my ear as he pounded into me...

Gods, what was wrong with me? How could I ever want that? What those men did to me had torn me apart each time, and yet I wanted... no, I needed it from Lhiam. I wanted him inside me like I wanted my next breath.

How was that possible?

And not only were Nibley and Dasan lovers, they were married, if I could believe Dasan's words of passion. Many places Master had dragged me to had had a sort of reluctant acceptance of same-sex relationships, but they were usually seen as a side-relationship. A man would marry a woman, beget offspring, and have a male lover on the side. In Master's troupe, there were two women who spent their lives together, as a husband and wife did, but they were often seen as outsiders, even in the carnival troupe. And gods forbid if they were seen being affectionate in a town. The one time a village person had seen the women kissing, while we passed through the village, we had been forced to leave early.

So was it possible that I had found myself in a country that accepted those kinds of relationships, to the point that they allowed marriage? I shivered as I looked up at the men, never wanting to be able to speak more than in that moment.

Maybe I could find them as a man and ask them. Ask them how it was possible that they had come to be so happy, so lucky.

But I kept myself silent and left them when their replacements came. As always, Dasan jokingly invited me home, and for the first time, I was tempted to accept and follow them. To see how two men who loved each other lived. But I refrained. The princess would wake soon, and I needed to be waiting outside her door when she did.

I had been in the castle for over two weeks when I followed Lacy as she went on a day-long "nature walk" picnic with 2 women, along with over twenty children, girls and boys. It was a sort of school that she told me her cousin, Lhiam, had begun for the town's children. Many of the townspeople refused to send their kids to the school, thinking that book learning wasn't as important as learning whatever trade their parents were passing onto them, but she told me she saw more and more children each day.

I followed at Lacy's heels, as always, amused at the antics of the children. When Lacy and I had first come up on the small schoolhouse, the children had all gone silent at the sight of me. Lacy had laughed at their hesitation, assuring them that I was "harmless." I grumbled at the descriptor, but sat patiently as she told me to sit, then ushered the children forward. A few brave children— two boys and one little girl— moved forward, their eyes on me. The little girl was the first to reach me. She reached forward, fingering my nose, before letting her fingers trail down my face to my neck. She petted me gently, whispering, "Nice doggy."

I frowned down at her but stayed still as the two boys gripped at the scruff around my neck as well. One of the boys was a little rough, but I didn't move as they explored my fur.

"He's so soft," one of them muttered. His words seemed to break the spell that had fallen over the children, for soon I was practically tackled as little hands worked into my fur, dug into my mouth, and poke my eyes. I huffed to get the kids out of my mouth, but kept my mouth open until their fingers were clear, so I wouldn't hurt them. I felt something, like new eyes on me, so I looked up and I almost jerked to my feet. Only the thought that the move would hurt some of the children who were climbing on my back kept me down.

Lhiam stood next to Lacy, staring down at me with something in his eyes I dared not decipher. It was amusement mixed with the softest of affection, and it set my heart to racing, a lump forming in my throat, as I stood slowly, letting a few of the children fall to the grass, giggling as they fell.

10- Settling In

----

* *I really love Edon. He's one of my favorite characters I've written haha**

LHIAM

Again, I seemed to have come upon an incredible sight. The same feeling of awe, affection, and amusement ran through my entire body as I stared down at Edon as it had that first time I saw him in the garden with Lacy, calmly resting as she read to him from a book of children's fairy tales.

He was completely swarmed with children. Most were young, under the age of 10, because their parents had no use for them until they were useful in their various occupations, but there were 3— 2 boys and a girl— who were a bit older than Lacy, maybe mid-teens. Even those older children touched Edon, petting him and crawling all over him.

"Is he a real wolf or is he part dog?" the older girl asked Lacy as she rubbed her fingers gently along Edon's ears. The wolf seemed to bask in the touch and pushed his head against the girl's hand.

The shooting irritation in my gut was not jealousy. Because I refused to be jealous of a 14-year-old girl.

"We're not sure, because we sort of adopted him," Lacy explained, looking down at Edon with a sort of apologetic frown on her lips. He didn't seem to notice, because one of the children, a boy who was barely 3, had fallen in his excitement and was holding back tears as he held his little injured hand to his chest.

Edon gently shook off a few of the children, bent his head down, and nuzzled his nose into the boy's chest, chuffing softly. The boy squealed in excitement, clapping his hands, and then leapt forward, digging his fingers in the fur around Edon's face. I could see the wolf flinch, and hear one of the two teacher's gasp, but he didn't lash out at the too-tight grip of the toddler. He simply straightened, setting the boy on his feet, before turning back to Lacy and returning to her side. The boy toddled after him, grabbing at his tail, chattering nonsensically, but Edon ignored him.

"But we're pretty sure he's full wolf," Lacy finished belatedly, her entire face alight as she stared me down. I tried to close myself off, because I could feel the gaze of the other two women, and I must look a sight— staring at the fucking wolf like he was my next meal.

Because gods, I wanted him. More and more each day, I had to fight the urge to find him and fuck him so hard he couldn't walk without thinking about me for a week. And the other, strange and new urges I had only felt for him. Like marking him with my scent, making sure that anyone who came across him knew to whom he belonged, to whom he returned each night. The possessive feelings of lust I felt for him were wholly new to me, and overwhelming.

"His mannerisms show wolf," one of the teen boys said knowingly, staring down into Edon's eyes. Edon looked back for a moment before turning up to look at Lacy. "That ain't no dog."

"That isn't a dog," one of the women corrected the boy, and he rolled his eyes.

"Well, it isn't," he muttered.

"Let's go," Lacy called as the women began to gather up the children. Edon began herding the smaller children, the ones who slipped through the teachers' hands and began to run the other way. The wolf loped after the small boy he had comforted before, whose name was Tay, if the yelling teacher was to be believed, and began to herd him back to the women. He used his lips, nipping at the boy's running heels, until the giggling boy was back before the women.

It went that way all the way up to the clearing Lacy had picked for the outing. I followed with two of my guards, trailing behind the group to watch for stragglers, as the two teachers taught the children about the trees they passed, the various bird sounds, and even some tracking tips and herbology. I knew my school was right now a sort of daycare for the younger children of overworked parents, rather than the true school I wanted, but I knew with time, the idea would grow, and I would eventually have my dream of multiple classes teaching many subjects, and even possibly sending some children off to the university in the Empire's capital.

Edon seemed to take a special interest in young Tay, or maybe the boy was just the most in need of the wolf, because after a while I noticed that the boy was actually riding on the small wolf's back, just between his shoulder blades. Edon seemed bemused, but I laughed out loud when I saw the boy, delightedly clapping his hands as he swayed on the wolf's back.

At my laugh, Edon turned back to me, huffing in indignation. But I saw the amusement in his eyes as he rolled them and then ran ahead towards the teachers.

We spent the entire day in the clearing, with the children naming the various bugs they saw, the teachers sending the older kids off to gather specific herbs or plants. It was a somewhat chaotic day, but I did manage to get Edon alone for a moment, just after lunch. The wolf had spent the entire lunchtime being begrudgingly fed by various tiny hands. The teachers, neither of whom seemed to care much for Edon, had warned the children not to feed the wolf, but none of them seemed to pay any attention to the women. Especially since Lacy was ripping off bits of her chicken and letting Edon gently nip them from her palms.

I found him by the small stream that ran around the clearing. He was lapping from it silently, and when I came upon him, his entire body tensed as his ears pricked towards me.

"I'm glad you seem to be settling in so well. I assume you've decided to stay?"

The wolf watched me, then chuffed and shrugged in that wolfy way he had. I smiled, shaking my head.

"Lacy has never had this much freedom. Usually it's a chore to figure out who has the time to take her where she wants to go, then they inevitably get bored, or she goes somewhere they don't want to go... It's just nice not to have to worry about her. Thank you."

Edon cocked his head, his eyes filled with disbelief. "No really, thank you," I assured him. "I know you'll keep her safe, so I'm not worried about her constantly like I was."

The wolf made a soft snorting sound, and then he met my eyes and I could almost hear the question he wanted to pose.

"I was hoping for... I wanted to ask you for a favor."

The wolf lifted a paw, stamping it down, as if demanding I continue.

"I have a council meeting tomorrow. It's with all of the members, all twelve. I'm sure I'll be fine, but I always like to have a little extra protection when there are that many... erm," I paused, unsure how to word snakes politely to the wolf, but he huffed in amusement, so I knew he understood what I didn't want to voice. "If I have you, I'll have that bit of extra protection, and no one will really realize it... I also have to go into town the next day, for the opening of a shelter I've been funding. I could use the extra protection then, too."

The wolf's acquiescence was almost instantaneous. He tilted his head and exposed his neck in submission. Something I had only seen him do to me and hadn't seen since those first few days he was here.

"Good," I mumbled, unsure if I liked that submission or not. I wanted his help if he wanted to give it; but I wanted him to have the choice. I wanted him to help me, to spend time with me, because he wanted to. Not because he felt he had to. "Thank you."

Edon tilted his head the other way, no doubt picking up on my hesitation, and I forced a smile.

What would it take for him to be as comfortable around me as he was with Lacy, or even how I had seen him with Tate? Would he ever be able to let himself go with me, or would he always see me as his "master?" How could I ever pursue with him what I wanted, when he treated me like a slave master?

11- Comforting Companion

E DON

I was ecstatic when Lhiam asked me to accompany him, to be by his side for the next two days. That thing I always felt when I thought of him— I wanted to pursue it. I wanted to know what it was. And I knew if I just spent a bit more time with him, I might be able to figure out what it was I felt whenever he was near. Whatever it was, it made me want to drop to my belly and submit, but at the same time, to jump upon him and claim ownership. I wanted my scent all over him, wanted to know what he smelled like aroused, what his eyes looked like as he came.

Gods, I wanted to taste him. I wanted to run my hands, and my tongue, all over his body. I wanted him to claim me, to leave his mark on me, just as I did on him. I wanted to shout to the world that he was mine. That I was his.

And it was all more than I could handle. I had never felt anything near to this, and it was overwhelming.

Especially since it was all impossible. Even if he did feel some kind of physical attraction to me, he was the prince of the realm. He couldn't possibly pursue more than something secret, hidden, carnal with me.

But with each passing day, a bit more of me was lost to him, so I began to believe that maybe I was alright with that. For now. If it was all he could give me, then it was all I would demand. Until I was inevitably forced to give him up.

But something told me that these feelings were only for him. That if I didn't pursue them with him, I would never feel them again.

And I didn't want to give that up. Not even for the fear that still pervaded my body when I thought of someone taking me that way, or the terror that cut off all thought when I thought of trusting him with my heart.

Because trust was not something someone as broken as me was able to give so easily.

Trust no one and they can't hurt you. Physically, they can break you. But your soul, and your heart, were safe. It was a lesson I learned early on, and one I clung to with abandon.

But giving this beautiful man my body was not giving in; it wouldn't break me, so long as I held myself at arm's length. So long as I kept him from burrowing even further into my heart.

The next morning, I woke at my normal time, but I was met at my door by Lhiam, backed by two guards. One I recognized as Robert, one of the night guards I had spent some time with. He was occasionally paired with Nibley, and they seemed to be friends. Robert smiled and patted my head as I moved to stand by Lhiam.

"You borrowing Lacy's wolf for the meeting, Your Highness?" Robert asked as he dug his fingers into my ears. I wanted to purr as the man's fingers scratched at a sensitive spot just next to my ear. I closed my eyes and pressed against his big palm, before opening them and turning to Lhiam. The prince glared down at me, heat and frustration heady in his eyes. But as quickly as I saw the emotions, he shuttered them, and I wondered if I had really seen them at all.

"He's a good guard, and most barely notice him." Lhiam's voice seemed dull, lifeless somehow.

"He is, sir," Robert answered, seemingly just as confused as me by Lhiam's sudden coldness. "He spends most nights with one of us out at the gates. He's a comforting companion to have."

Lhiam's eyes were on me again, but I tried to ignore him as I walked by his side. I could feel his concern, and his confusion, but I tuned it out. He was wondering why I didn't sleep. There was no way I was going to explore my nightmares with him.

They belonged in my mind, and I could handle them myself. There was no need to drag the prince into my own personal hell.

When we entered the large meeting room, there was a hush of voices as twelve men, all sitting around a large oak table, stood at attention at Lhiam's entrance. The prince moved to the largest chair at the head of the table, ignoring the few whispers around him at my presence, and then sat. I moved to his side, looking around at the men around me. Most were in their mid-to-late-sixties, but three were younger. Only five bore weapons, and from the looks of the calluses on their hands, and the scars on their bodies, I could tell only two knew how to use them. I watched those two closely, knowing they were the only real physical threats in the room. The others would back down if I growled loudly or bared my teeth.

The meeting began when the prince called attention to the room and all of the men sat. Robert and the other guard stood a few feet back from Lhiam, but I remained at his side. A little cushion had been set next to the chair, and I was amused by the simple gesture, musing on how my life had changed so much in such a short amount of time. Most of my life I had slept on wooden floors in dirty inns, or the ground around a fire, and then later on in a cage not fit for an animal. Now I was being given a silky, warm cushion so I wouldn't have to sit directly on the thick fur rug beneath the table.

I sat on the cushion but didn't lie down and rest. I sat up straight, staring the men down around me. I could tell I unnerved a few of the men, but I was glad for that. If they were afraid of me, it would lessen any kind of danger Lhiam was in.

I completely tuned out their words as they spoke of crops, military troops, ships, stores for the coming winter, and various other things that made me yawn more than once. After what felt like an eternity, but what I knew must have been only an hour at most, Lhiam looked over at me, winking.

"You can lay down to rest, Edon," he whispered so that only I would hear. "This is a ridiculously long meeting. You're going to get sore sitting up like that."

I whined quietly, pressing my nose against his hand, and he froze. He watched me, insecurity flashing in his eyes, before his smile deepened, softened, and he gently began to rub at my ears. I sighed, pressing my head against his hand, reveling against his warm touch. His breathing hitched, but he soon turned his attention back to the meeting. He kept his hand on my head, however, rubbing at my ears and gently petting my head. I laid my muzzle on his thigh, wanting to smile when his hand twitched and his body heat shot up. But he didn't make any other motion that the move had affected him. He simply continued to rub my head, down my neck, occasionally scratching at my ears.

I managed to doze a few times, and I was amazed that each time I woke, Lhiam still pressed his hand against me. Even if it was just to lay it on my head. The closeness, the intimacy I felt with him was affecting me. I could feel my chest constricting, and it sent fear down my spine.

I couldn't let him in. I couldn't. I wouldn't survive it when he inevitably betrayed me. When his seeming fascination with a new toy came to an end.

12- Pack

L HIAM

Edon's big head on my lap was infuriatingly distracting. I rubbed his soft fur, amused by the annoyed looks of a few of the council members. The same ones who continued to demand that I force Lacy to get rid of Edon. They were a part of the reason I had brought him today. So that they were aware that Edon was mine as much as he was Lacy's.

More so.

Mine.

The wolf's little exhalations as he slept, his gentle, warm breaths against the skin of my hand, against my thighs, was like warning bells in my mind.

I was falling so far for this little wolf man, I couldn't even remember not having these all-encompassing thoughts distracting me.

When we adjourned for lunch, a few of the councilors moved towards me. One— Rafael, who was one of the younger council members, and one of the ones I didn't want to strangle on a daily basis— laughed loudly when Edon growled as he neared. I looked down at Edon, unsure why he was reacting that way, when I noticed the sword at Rafael's waist. Since the man was a former Empire general, and currently my general, he was one of the only men who routinely carried weapons on his person.

Edon had obviously picked him out as one of the true threats in the room. And he didn't like him coming so near me.

I pushed down the warmth that spread through my chest at his protectiveness and held my hand up to him to try to quiet him. Edon lifted his head from my lap, continuing to bare his teeth to the general, but the man didn't stop his advance.

"Edon," I murmured. "It's alright. He's a friend. Calm, sweetheart."

My words seemed to mollify the wolf, because he shut his muzzle and quieted, but he was still on high alert, and he moved to my other side, so he stood between me and the general.

"Damn, how did you get a wolf trained like that?" Rafael asked as he reached out and shook my hand in greeting. He acted like Edon didn't begin to bare his teeth again when his hand was only a few inches from the wolf's teeth. "He protects you like you're pack."

I looked down at Edon and smiled gently when he met my eyes. I could almost see the words in his mind. Or maybe it was just my own selfish hope that he was thinking my pack.

"Lacy and I rescued him from... a rather terrible situation. He's become family," I answered truthfully, and I could see Edon's ears twitching. With pride? Joy? I couldn't tell. He watched Rafael far too closely.

"That's incredible. You're lucky. Wolves are fiercely loyal, and they put pack above all else, including their own lives. If he's adopted you into his pack, you've got a fierce protector for life."

I nodded, not sure if I liked that he would put my life above his own, but I liked the idea that he thought of me as his family.

Rafael's talk turned to the troops he was training near his home in the south, and I let my hand drift down to Edon again. This time, he seemed a bit more relaxed as I ran my hand up and down his neck. I barely noticed when Rafael stopped talking.

"He's all but purring," Rafael whispered, as if not to disturb Edon. I looked down at the wolf, and sure enough, his eyes were closed, and he was leaning into me, his chest visibly vibrating with pleasure.

I smiled when the wolf's eyes drifted open and he lazily looked up and met my eyes.

Gods those eyes would be the death of me.

It was another five hours after lunch before the insipid councilors allowed the meeting to end. I was exhausted but determined to follow through with my dinner plans. Having spent the entire day around people, I needed to be alone. I allowed Robert and Cain to follow me to the kitchens, then to help me carry the dinner I had asked chef to prepare for me out into my favorite garden— the one I'd had Edon brought to his first day here. When they had set up the little picnic on the ground, I dismissed them, telling them I was perfectly safe in the castle walls, in the out-of-the-way garden, with my canine protector.

But the moment they were gone, I pulled a shirt and breeches from the bottom of the basket and motioned to Edon.

"Can you shift, please? Your quiet nature is appealing right now, because I am in need of tranquility and solitude after today, but I would like some conversation."

The wolf cocked his head, then moved forward, taking the clothes from me gently in his mouth and trotting back towards the thin grove of trees. I heard shuffling, then the rustling of clothes, then he poked his head around a tree and moved towards me. I always marveled at the graceful, loping way he moved. Even in his human form, he advanced with the elegance of a wild animal, like he was stalking his prey. He was also completely silent on his bare feet as he moved towards me, his dark hair flopping in his eyes as he cocked his head down at me.

I patted the blanket next to me, leaning back against the tree behind me. It was a small fruit tree, its branches empty of leaves due to the late autumn weather.

"That's better," I whispered, keeping my voice soft so he wouldn't spook. But he seemed much more confident, more sure of himself, than the last time I had spent any kind of time alone with him. He simply met my eyes, nodding, and accepted the plate of steak, gravy and biscuits I handed to him.

"Thank you, Your Highness," he said as he took the plate, and I flinched at the title. This was truly the first time I had spoken to him since the day when he had told me his name. Most of the other times I had seen him, he had been in his wolf form. His voice was rough with disuse, like it had been that day he had first spoken in the gods-only-knew-how-long, but there was a softness, a tenderness to it now that, by the gods, went straight to my groin.

"Please," I said immediately. "Please call me Lhiam. At least... at least when we're alone."

Edon cocked his head in that way that made him look so much like a wolf, and then his lips were splitting into the softest of smiles.

"Of course, Lhiam," he breathed, and it was all I could do not to lean forward and brush my mouth across his lips. To taste my name on his breath. I clenched my hands into fists in my lap to hold myself back, and his eyes flicked to them, along with a heady fear. He watched my hands like I may lash out at him at any moment.

"Sorry," I muttered, relaxing my hands and reaching for my own plate. His eyes met mine again, and I saw the question there. I hesitated, unsure how to phrase what I wanted so badly to convey to him. "Edon, I need you to know... I would never— never— hurt you. You don't need to be wary of me, because I would sooner..." I paused, because he was smiling again, that soft, hesitant, unsure smile that forced my mind to a screeching halt.

"I know," he said, and then he shifted, as if finding time to pinpoint his words. "It is habit, to be wary of clenched fists. To watch for anger. To flinch at loud noises, or sudden movements. But I am getting better. I am sorry; it is not you, Lhiam."

It was the most I had ever heard him say, and each word was breathy, rough, and for the first time, I could hear a slight accent in a few of his words. Lilting, and yet harsh. But I was unable to place it.

"That's...that's good. I'm glad you're healing."

His head tilted, and the smile was replaced by a grimace of self-deprecation. I laughed, somehow knowing exactly what the reaction was for.

"Don't worry. It will come. The mind and heart heal much slower than the body. It will just take time, and patience."

"I am glad I have both," he sighed, looking away as he pressed his fork into his meat and pushed it around the plate.

"Eat, please," I pushed, unsure why his words were so unsure, so... lost sounding.

We sat in silence as we ate. Edon didn't seem to mind or be self-conscious at all whenever I caught him staring at me. It was amusing to me every time I noticed something about him that was so very... wolf. Like the way he stared me down, obviously watching each move of my body with appreciation, but didn't care that I noticed. There was no shame, only a heady desire. And I was eternally grateful that he finally seemed to be moving past the fear of me, possibly of men in general, and that he might consider something more with me. Because if the fire in his eyes was any judge, he wanted me. Possibly as much as I did him.

His movements, even as he ate, were also reminiscent of a wolf, even the way he breathed as he stared up at the setting sun made me think of a wolf at rest: long, slow, deliberate. But I knew he was ready to spring up at any moment.

He was hesitant with the fork and knife, and that was the only thing he seemed to be embarrassed about. He blushed heavily after the fifth time he dropped the fork in trying to use it to hold the steak still while he cut it. He held the fork and glared down at the steak, as if it was some monster he had to vanquish, and I couldn't help but laugh. He looked up at me, hurt in his eyes, but I shook my head. I set my own fork and knife down on the blanket and lifted the steak from my plate to my lips. I bit into it, laughing when the gravy dripped down my chin.

Edon chuckled, the sound quiet and withdrawn, staring at me with horri-fied fascination, before he raised his own steak to his lips and began to eat it with gusto. When our steaks were gone, we licked our fingers clean of the gravy, and I used my biscuits to scrape up the last of the gravy on my plate. Edon watched me before emulating, and he grinned wolfishly at me, his head tilting, and I could almost picture his ears perking.

We set the plates on the blankets, and I leaned back against the tree behind me, my hands on my stomach. Edon's breathy little pants were like a lullaby to me as I leaned my head back and closed my eyes. The sun had set, and the chill in the air was offset by Edon's warmth as his knees brushed against mine. I could feel him watching me, but I forced myself to ignore him. I couldn't push him more than what he was comfortable, and today was the first time we had spent more than a few minutes together.

I couldn't push him and risk losing him altogether.

"Lhiam," he inquired, his voice so quiet I almost didn't hear it. "May I ask you something? Lacy has answered many of my questions about life in Teren, the Empire, the council... everything I needed to know about life here. But there are a few things I am curious about that I can't ask her."

I raised my eyebrows and nodded, keeping my eyes closed and my head back. I felt him move, and I stiffened when I felt his warmth at my side. He pressed himself against me, laying down and staring up at the appearing stars, his head firmly resting against my left thigh. I stared down at him for a moment, flabbergasted, before I righted myself and tried to calm my racing heart.

"Of course," I managed to gasp out, praying his hearing while he was in human form wasn't as powerful as I knew it was as a wolf. I didn't want him to hear how fast my heart was beating at the simple act of trust and affection he had shown me. "I'll do my best to answer any questions you have."

"There are two guards who work overnight. I join them sometimes when I... when I can't sleep." I nodded, urging him to continue. My hands were clenched into fists, to keep them from reaching out and rubbing my fingers through his hair. Gods it looked soft. He continued to stare up at the stars and the rising moon, but I could see his fingers twitching on his chest, tugging at one of the buttons nervously.

"They are lovers...No," he said, shaking his head. The movement sent vibrations up my body and I held back a groan as my semi-hard cock pressed itself into full hardness. Gods, I hoped it was too dark for him to see it. "I believe they are married. They only know me as a wolf, so I can't ask them. But I came upon them..." he broke off, a blush rising in his cheeks and then he smiled softly. "I heard one call the other 'husband.'"

I hesitated, waiting for the question, but when he wasn't forthcoming with his confusion, I took a guess.

"You are wondering if they're really married? I can find out for you," I answered, unsure if I was jealous that he wanted to know about another man's relationship or confused that he didn't seem to be asking about only one of the men, but both.

"No," he answered quickly, taking a deep breath and then letting it out slowly. "Well, yes. I'm wondering if that's possible. I've never heard of marriage between two men. Is it possible, for one man to marry another?"

I froze completely, terrified that I may say the wrong thing. "It depends on the region, I suppose. In Teren, marriages between two men or two women are recognized by the government. They have been for generations. But other places in the Empire, same-sex couples can be looked down on, even persecuted. The Emperor is a staunch supporter of legalizing same-sex marriage in all of the kingdoms, but there are many that oppose that. Of the twelve countries, only 3 recognize same-sex marriages, and there are still 4 in which it is staunchly illegal to even be in that kind of relationship."

I paused, hoping I didn't scare him, but when I looked down, he was smiling that hesitant, small smile I was growing to be absolutely obsessed with.

"That's good. They seemed very much in love. I'm glad they are allowed their happiness."

I stared down at him, my mouth open in awe, and shook my head.

"You are an incredible man, Edon," I whispered, finally giving up and running my fingers through his hair. He pressed his head up against my hand, closing his eyes in contentment, and then his weight was off my lap and I had to fight the protest that rose to my throat at the loss.

When I looked up at him, he was staring at me, his eyes shining in the light from the moon.

"Lhiam," he whispered, and I jerked forward, the needy desperation in his voice drawing me to him like a moth to flame. I only hoped the burn would be worth it.

Because this man had my heart in the palm of his hand. And I dreaded the day he may leave me. The day he may decide that being with a prince wasn't all jewels and parties. It was the constant fear of death, and the annoyance of never-ending meetings and simpering politicians. It was the opposite of the freedom I knew had to be so important to him.

I lifted my hand, letting my forefinger trace his upper lip, and then drawing my thumb across his lower lip, back and forth. He shivered, and I could tell from the heat wafting from him that it wasn't due to the cold. He stared at me, his eyes wide, desire and hesitation heady in his every move.

"Edon," I murmured, kneeling up so I was towering over him. I let my hand cup his face, the other dropping down to settle on his hip. "I want to kiss you. May I? May I kiss you, sweetheart?"

Edon barely had the chance to nod before I was on him. I had to hold myself back from completely devouring him. I knew that this may be his first real kiss, and I didn't want to overwhelm him. I wanted only perfection for my beautiful wolf.

I pressed my lips to his, tilting my head to get better access. He froze in my arms, a small inhalation my only indication that he was enjoying my touch. I held myself still for a few moments, letting him become accustomed to the feel of my lips on his, my warmth mingling with his, before I began to press my mouth against his in a slow sort of dance.

He sighed, finally relaxing into my arms, and I smiled against his lips at the small victory. My hands shook as I held both up, clutching his face in both palms, holding him against me as I deepened the kiss. I opened my mouth, sucking at first his top lip, then his bottom, nibbling gently at the fuller bottom lip. When he gasped again, I took advantage and gently moved my tongue into his mouth. I ran my tongue over his teeth, shivering when I felt that the canines were sharper and longer than the others, something I hadn't noticed before, and then, when he opened his mouth further to admit me, I lapped at his tongue.

I sucked on his tongue, drawing a stunning whimper from him, and dragged it back into my mouth. I let him explore, holding back a bit as he tentatively raised his hands, clutching at the tunic at my chest as his tongue arched up along the top of my mouth.

I gasped, my chest heaving, as I pulled away, chuckling when he tried to follow, his eyes still closed as his mouth sought out mine. I moved my hands so that one clutched at the hair at the nape of his neck, and the other rested against his neck, my thumb running along his pulse point. His chest was heaving even more violently than mine, his lips swollen and wet, his eyes dazed and filled with lust as he finally opened them and set them on me. He made a noise, a mix between a growl and a whine, and I could feel my smile deepen.

"I need..." I paused, rubbing circles against his neck to try to calm him. He was on his knees, leaning back against his ankles, but I could see his hips rocking, thrusting rhythmically, and I knew if I didn't hurry, I was going to lose control. "Edon, I need you to pay attention right now, alright?"

The whine/growl rose from his chest again, but he nodded, his hands clenching and unclenching at my chest as he met my eyes. His were still filled with an overwhelming lust and desire, but there was clarity there. It would have to be enough.

"I need to know that if I ever do anything you don't like, or if you are ever uncomfortable, you will tell me. I need you to know that you can say no to me, anytime, and I'll stop. I don't care who I am, or what you think you should do, what you think I expect from you, or what you think you owe me. You tell me no, and I will stop, no matter what. Do you understand? You do not owe me anything, especially not your body. Please remember, your body is yours, and you are free to do with it what you want."

His eyes darkened for a moment, his fingers freezing against my chest, before he nodded.

"I understand, Lhiam," he whispered huskily, and gods, his voice was like a caress up my cock.

"I never want to be another thing that keeps you from sleeping, sweetheart," I murmured, tugging on the back of his neck to draw him back to me.

13- Keeps You From Sleeping

EDON

"I never want to be another thing that keeps you from sleeping, sweetheart."

My entire body melted into his arms at his words. My mind was screaming at me to pull away. I was so overwhelmed with sensation, it was all I could do to hold myself upright. My cock was leaking heavily in my loose breeches, harder than it had ever been, and Lhiam hadn't even touched it. He had only kissed me and I was a mewling, drooling mess in his arms.

No. Not kissed me. What he was doing to me couldn't be called a kiss in any language. He was devouring me. Marking me. Burning me from the inside out. Making me wholly his, with agonizing swipes of his tongue and grazes of his teeth against my lips. Every time he drew my tongue into his mouth, and then bit down lightly, my entire body jerked, lightning shooting down my spine, and another drop of pre-cum dribbled down my cock. I could feel my hips jerking, humping the empty air, wanting nothing more than to feel pressure against my engorged appendage, but I couldn't stop myself, or even force myself to care.

Everything I was, belonged to Lhiam. I couldn't escape him, even if I wanted to.

And gods, the last thought on my mind was escape.

I wanted to crawl inside him, inside his kiss, and never leave. I wasn't just warm, I felt safe, protected, desired, needed. In those moments, he needed me, just as much as I needed him.

And it was a heady feeling.

After what felt like an eternity in his arms, Lhiam was falling back, dragging me with him. He leaned his back against the small tree and led me down to straddle his hips. I gasped when I finally felt friction against my cock when his hardness rubbed up against my own.

"Tell me you want this, Edon. Tell me you want me to make you come."

I humped against him mindlessly a few times before his hands were on my hips, holding me still as he chuckled against my neck. His tongue flicked out, tasting my pulse, before he let his teeth graze over it and I cried out, stiffening as unbearable heat pooled low in my belly.

"Tell me you want this, Edon. I need to hear you say it."

I shivered and whimpered pathetically, unable to find the words for what felt like minutes as I thrust my cock against empty air. Finally, I managed to gasp out, "Want you. Need you. Please, Lhiam."

He pulled back, studying my face for a moment, and I returned the favor as I glared down at him. His hair was mussed, and I tried to remember when I had grabbed at it. His lips were swollen and wet, his face flushed, his pupils blown, and there was a bruised looking bite mark on his neck. I didn't even remember leaving it, but a rush of pride and rightness went through my body at the sight.

Mine. He's mine.

I fingered the mark, and I knew I was probably smiling like an idiot, because a soft smile quirked on Lhiam's lips.

"My sexy wolf is a biter," he chuckled, and then his mouth was back on mine and I lost all sense of myself again. All I knew was his heat, his skin against mine, his fingers yanking my shirt off. Then my pants were down around my thighs, his hands were gone, and I was left to nibble and suck and whimper against his ear while he fiddled with something, groaning as I pressed my tongue into his ear.

When he pressed something hard, wet and hot against my erect cock I cried out, yanking my head back to stare down at my groin. He held both of our cocks against each other in one large palm. I was thick but shorter than he was, and I gulped when I saw his size. He was huge, possibly the biggest I had seen, and thick. I reached down, fingering the wet head, and I felt him inhale on a gasp as I pressed my finger into the precum beading at his tip. I lifted my finger to my mouth, meeting his eyes as I brought the drop to my mouth. His mouth hung open, panting as he watched me.

Ever since I had seen Dasan and Nibley, I had wondered why Dasan had tasted his and Nibley's cum. And I had wondered why the sight had so intrigued me.

Now I thought I understood. There was something primal, almost animalistic, in tasting Lhiam's essence. It was a claiming; like I was showing him that he belonged to me, even if it was just in that moment. Because in that moment, he was a part of me, and I a part of him. I was tasting his very body.

I barely tasted anything, just a hint of salt, but the look in his eyes made it worth it. He stared up at me like he wanted to devour me, and I shivered because I wanted him to. Needed him to.

He growled, slamming his lips against mine and shoving his tongue into my mouth as he gripped my ass and drew me forward. I hadn't noticed when he unbuttoned his own shirt, so I was pleasantly surprised when our cocks rubbed up against each other, surrounded by the heat of both of our naked bellies. I thrust against him, starting up a steady rhythm he somehow managed to control with his fingernails digging into my ass.

I could feel myself mumbling nonsense into his mouth, along with whimpers, gasps, and moans, but he stayed almost calm. He watched me, his eyes bright with lust, as I humped erratically against his cock, feeling his hardness pulsing against my own.

"Lhiam," I breathed as I pulled away from his mouth and shoved my lips against his neck. I held onto his head, completely wrapping myself around him as my body jerked involuntarily. I could feel the heat in my lower belly beginning to throb, and I knew I wouldn't last much longer.

But I feared the fall. Because with each breath in, the accumulation was more than I had ever felt before, in the few times I had been allowed pleasure by my first Master or was forced to feel pleasure by the men my second Master allowed to have me. This was so, so much more. It was like comparing a candle flame to lightning.

And I feared the lightning would change me forever. It would destroy me and leave me broken and in pieces that I didn't know how to put back together.

"Lhiam...?" I whined breathlessly, as another wave of ecstasy built up and still I hadn't peaked. "Lhiam, need... need you," I mouthed against his neck. I had no idea what to ask, how to voice my fear, my agony, but he seemed to understand anyway.

"You ready to come, little wolf?" he asked, his own words coming out in panting spurts as he thrust up against me each time I humped forward. "Can you come for me, sweetheart? I want to see you fall apart for me. Can you do that for me?"

I cried out at his words, the intensity building, building, building, before I finally felt myself shatter and I screamed. His mouth pressed against mine, holding my cries back, swallowing them before they drew others into our little bubble. My mind went white as my body broke completely and I was left a quivering mess in Lhiam's arms.

I jerked against him for an eternity, feeling my hot cum easing the way even further between our cocks as I continued to shudder against him. And soon, heat enveloped my cock as his own spurted against mine and he was grunting into my mouth, sipping at my lips as he lost himself to his own orgasm.

When I finally came down, I was lying completely limp against him below me. My face was pressed against his neck as he rubbed his fingers through my hair. His words came to me slowly as I drifted in a lazy, post-coital bliss that had my entire body shivering as aftershocks ran up and down my spine.

"Shh, little wolf," he murmured as he stroked my head, his other hand rubbing up and down my back in soothing circles. "Rest now. I've got you. I've got you, sweetheart."

Please like and comment if you liked it (or if you didn't-- let me know why!) :):):)

14- What a Fall

LHIAM

If I had thought I knew what sex was before the last half hour, I was a fool. I hadn't even penetrated Edon, nor he me, but the orgasm he had given me with his uncertain touches, his inexperienced thrusts, and his soft whimpers in my ear had completely changed everything I had ever thought I knew about sex.

He had torn my world apart and flipped me around completely.

And as he lay in my arms, his breaths just starting to slow into little hiccupping whimpers, his body limp against me, I prayed that I had done the same for him.

When his climax had been building, his body beginning to twitch and jerk sporadically against mine, I had felt his fear. I had almost pulled away, even, but one look at his face as I dragged him away from my neck, to ensure he still wanted to continue, and I knew I had to keep going. Because the desperation and fear in his eyes was almost wholly superseded by the need, the lust, and dear gods, the affection he felt in those moments.

And then I asked him to come, and he had completely broken apart in my arms. I had watched him for as long as I could, slamming my mouth against his to keep his scream from drawing any guards towards us, but I soon had to follow him down. His wet heat hitting my chest, my stomach, and dripping down to my cock had been too much to resist, and I allowed myself to jump from the ledge and join him at the bottom.

And gods, what a fall.

Now I held him tightly, whispering soothing words into his ears, and I could feel the exact moment he came back into himself fully, because he stiffened just a bit, pulled away, and stared into my eyes. His expression was shuttered, so I could feel my insecurity rising, because I couldn't tell if he was happy, angry, afraid...

And then he smiled, the motion filled with a mischievous kind of amusement, as he reached down between us and put his finger in our joined juices. I was left speechless as he scooped up just a bit, coating two fingers, and then brought his fingers up to my lips. I brought the digits into my mouth without hesitation, drawing out a surprised gasp from Edon as he stared with concentration at my lips. I sucked on his hot skin, tasting our joined cum and swallowing it down, before allowing his fingers freedom after one final lick.

I remembered the way he had tasted my precum, with his eyes alight with curiosity, and something dark, hesitant, and almost angry. As if doing it was an act of defiance. I wondered if I would ever understand why that was.

I wondered if I wanted to understand.

He cocked his head, and I smiled and put my mouth to his in a chaste kiss. "Delicious," I breathed against his mouth, and he sighed and chuckled, the sound rumbling up from deep in his belly.

He pulled back and jerked his head down to our joined bellies, and I understood immediately. I could sense this was a sort of defiance for him, but again, I didn't understand why. But I didn't have to. It was for him, and if it was what he wanted, I would help him scream his defiance to the world.

I ran my fingers through our joined, cooling juices, then lifted them to his mouth. He hesitated, and I could see a war waging behind his eyes, but then he was staring into my eyes and he was opening his mouth to draw my fingers in. He nipped and sucked at my fingers as I shuddered beneath him, and then he let them out and a discerning look crossed his eyes.

"Not delicious," he whispered, and I chuckled at the bemusement in his voice. "But I like it," he said simply.

We used one of the dinner napkins, wetted in the garden fountain, to clean the rest of our release from our bodies. Then we dressed, packed up the dinner, and moved back into the castle. I knew wolves were tactile creatures, and I had seen Lacy petting and fondling Edon plenty when he had been in his wolf form, but nothing could have prepared me for how affectionate he became post-orgasm. I had to fight everything in me not to push him down and have my way with him again. His body brushed against mine as we picked up the dinner dishes, his hands fingered my lips when I smiled down at him, as if tracing the shape of my smile, he ran his lips along my jawline when I bent to pick up the basket. It was as if he was trying to find any excuse to touch me— and he found plenty. His hands gripped mine as we walked down the hallway, dropping our dinner dishes off outside the kitchens. His body pressed against my side, his breaths were practically in my ear.

But the moment we came into more populated areas of the castle as we made our way to our rooms, he yanked himself away from me, just moments before a couple of guards rounded the corner. I felt a brief stab of pain when he pulled himself so totally away from me, but I understood. Many men felt shame in their desires for other men. I couldn't possibly expect Edon, who was barely learning how to navigate human society, to be that open and to allow himself to be seen as even more different.

Because while same-sex partnerships were legal in Teren, even allowing for marriage, they were not exactly accepted. There was still the question of children, and more traditional people saw those relationships as abnormal. So while I had never hidden my proclivities towards men, I knew I couldn't expect Edon to simply be alright with allowing the world to know he was even more different than he already was.

I would have to practice patience. Give him time to adjust.

When we stopped just outside his door, I pulled him to a stop before he could open it. I paused, looking around to ensure no one was around, listening closely just in case someone was coming around the corner. Then I leaned forward, brushing my lips against his in a chaste, warm kiss.

"Good night, little wolf. See you tomorrow?" I whispered against his lips, waiting for a moment for his nod before forcing myself away and down the hall.

Thanks for reading, darlings. Let me know what you think!

15- Dasan and Nibley

✱ *I'm not able to update as frequently as I would like. Ah, such is life...

I promise the story is completed; it's just getting on to update is like climbing a mountain sometimes... As always, please comment, comment, comment :):):):) **

EDON

The care Lhiam showed me as he cleaned my body of our joined release made my entire chest tighten to the point I feared I might not be able to take another breath. I watched him silently as we cleaned up from our dinner, and then walked towards the kitchens. I leaned against him, taking in his scent, the feel of his body moving against mine, his hand in mine hot and a little wet with sweat. I reveled in the way his breath ticked up when I brushed against him, and my wolf was ecstatic that I was so close to another. That I was touching, being touched.

But when I heard guards rounding the corner in front of us, I was jerked back to reality. Back to the reality that Lhiam was a prince, second only to the Emperor, and I was an orphan who couldn't even claim to be human. I pulled myself away, knowing that was what Lhiam would want, and what he was probably about to do himself. So I pulled away before he could, because it hurt less that way, somehow.

At least, that was what I told myself.

If Lhiam did want me, it was in the bedchamber, and in darkened corners; in secret. And for now, I had to be alright with that. Until he grew bored of his new toy, or until I got up the strength to move on.

Or until he had broken me past the point of caring.

When we stopped in front of my door, I hurriedly began to open it, fully expecting him to follow me inside, to take me like I knew he wanted to, but he stopped me with a hand on my arm. He looked around, and I realized he was making sure no one was around.

I flinched when a small piece of my heart sheared off at the realization.

His kiss was tender, soft, and heartbreaking.

Was he saying goodbye? Was that all, just tonight, that I got with him? I thought I would at least have a full night, maybe a few. But was he already cutting me loose? Gods, my chest felt like something heavy was pressing against it.

"Good night, little wolf. See you tomorrow?"

I nodded against him, willing to agree to anything if it meant I got to see him again. Got to feel his hands on me again. Got to feel his lips pressed against mine, his tongue battling with my own.

He disappeared, and I was left with his scent on my skin, and my mind and heart in chaos.

How had I allowed myself to fall so far?

I didn't even bother trying to sleep that night, knowing that sleep would be impossible with the way my mind was reeling and my heart refused to calm down.

I shifted to my wolf and made my way through the halls, finding Dasan and Nibley outside of the eastern gates. Both men greeted me with smiles, and Nibley leaned down to pet me between my ears.

"Hi, little wolf," the man grunted as he straightened again. "I don't have any bones for you tonight, sorry."

I huffed and lay down by the man's side, watching the road that stretched into the town below. The men were silent for a few minutes, their eyes alert to the darkness around them, before they seemed to start up a conversation I had perhaps interrupted with my presence.

"Naw," Dasan said suddenly, shaking his head and snorting. "I disagree. I think our prince would do it, if for no other reason than to anger that council of his. He doesn't even try to hide his distaste for them."

"It doesn't matter how much he hates them. If they denied his marriage, he couldn't go through with it. Not without their approval."

"This is all speculation anyways," Dasan said stubbornly. "It was one time he was seen with the boy. It's not as if he's proposed."

"You didn't see them," Nibley said gently, his eyes faraway. I began to pay attention to their conversation, sensing they were now speaking of me. "The way he looked at that boy. Gods, Dasan, the rest of the world didn't exist to them. Neither even noticed me."

Dammit, I hadn't noticed him. When had he seen us? Would Lhiam be angry that we had been seen together? I prayed that only Nibley had seen us, but those hopes were quickly dashed with his next words.

"And I wasn't the only one. The talk's all over the keep, because a few kitchen maids saw them, as well as a chambermaid, and you know how they talk. I worry for the boy. He looked young, inexperienced probably. Being in a relationship with royalty can't be easy..."

"One way or another, I'm just happy the prince has found someone," Dasan cut in. "He's always been loyal to his blood, to the country, fighting in his father's wars, raising his little cousin, putting himself last. It's good to see him finally finding some bit of happiness. And the gossipers will talk, so let them. They have good reason to. The prince has never been seen in any kind of relationship with another, man or woman. Many were starting to wonder if he was capable, if you catch my meaning."

I snorted softly, remembering Lhiam coming apart beneath me earlier that night, and all of the times I had felt his body reacting to mine.

No, he was more than capable.

Nibley eyed me, but he turned his attention back to the darkness around him and shook his head. "I'm happy for him as well. It's good to see him happy. He's definitely been different lately. Lighter. And he watches that boy like..."

"Like I watch you," Dasan finished, smirking smugly when Nibley blushed.

"Yes, exactly like. But there's something else there. He's holding back. Maybe because of the boy's age? I can't think it's his status– he is Tate's cousin, after all."

"Makes me want to meet the kid who stole the prince's heart," Dasan laughed, shifting his feet. "The boy who's got the high ruler of the realm wrapped around his finger."

Nibley chuckled, his hand reaching down to pet my head unconsciously. I wished I could tell them all their speculation was for nothing. They shouldn't even know about me and Lhiam. I was the prince's dirty plaything, and would never be anything more. I couldn't be. I was filthy; I was so much less than what he deserved. But for now, I was what he wanted. That was all. Their talk of love, and marriage, and acceptance was all for naught.

"The wolf seems sort of down tonight, don't you think?" Nibley whispered, as if trying to make sure I didn't hear. He bent down, scratching beneath my muzzle to bring my eyes up to his. I refused to meet his eyes, staring behind him and sighing as pain lanced through my chest at my own thoughts. "What's wrong, boy?"

I huffed gently, pulling away from the man, and standing to leave.

"Aww, you made him leave, Nibs," Dasan joked at my back. "You can't go asking a man how he's feeling. It's not masculine to have emotions, you know."

I didn't sleep at all that night. I simply laid down on the balcony just outside my room that overlooked the forest beyond the keep, and prayed that someday I would have the strength to leave and never look back. Because this pain in my heart, causing physical pain in my entire body, was more agony than either of my masters had ever been able to inflict.

Lhiam was waiting for me again the next morning, and he merely smiled down at me, a brightness to his eyes that had my ears twitching forward. I wanted to leap forward and rub my body all over him, mark him with my scent so any who scented him knew he was mine, but I held back.

Because he wasn't mine. And he never could be.

All night I had mulled over that knowledge, and it caused no less pain now than it had when I first realized it.

I followed him closely as he led the way to the stables, backed by two guards. I again recognized Robert, but the second guard was one I had never met before. He was young, maybe a couple of years older than me, but there was something in his eyes that marked him as older. Colder than he should be at that age. Robert called him Cain.

I had only been near the stables a few times, since Lacy usually preferred to walk everywhere we went, and I had never been inside. Knowing the horses would panic if they saw me near their home, I stayed just outside the large stable doors until Lhiam, Robert and Cain came back out.

As we made our way through the city streets, I stuck as close to Lhiam's stallion as the horse would allow. All three of the men's horses were large warhorses, and as such they seemed much calmer than some of the pack horses I had come across as a wolf. But they each still watched me out of the corner of their eye, their ears twitching, wary. I tried to keep my attention on the townspeople around us as we walked, but my attention continued to be drawn inexplicably back to Lhiam.

The way he had looked last night as he came. The way he smiled up at me, sleepy and sated, as our release cooled on our bodies. The tender way he helped me to dress and wiped my body down. I couldn't seem to get the images out of my mind.

Once we reached the home— a large building with 13 rooms that Lhiam had built for the elderly with no family to care for them and orphans, which he called Sunflower Manor— I stuck so close to Lhiam's side he tripped over me twice. He laughed it off, but I could feel my tail digging into my belly and my ears flattening against my head in apology. But I was unable to move too far away from him. Fear for him warred with an equally strong sense of needing to be as close to him as possible, and it was only because he learned to dance around me that he didn't trip more than twice.

There was a crowd of townspeople, probably the ones who had helped build Sunflower Manor, that Lhiam was thanking, shaking their hands, chatting, and laughing along with something one had said. His guards stood off a ways, their attention on the crowd around him. Just in front of the building were a man and a woman, husband and wife, who would run the home, caring for the children and elderly. And surrounding the couple were 5 children— I assumed they were the orphans. I recognized two of them as two children that were always at the school Lacy frequently visited, one of them the young boy Tay. When he saw me, he cried out "doggie!" and to the crowd's horror, he leapt at me. I stiffened, aware of the many weapons in the crowd that could be used against me if anyone feared for the child's safety.

I looked up, seeing Lhiam watching me as the crowd took a collective breath. I snorted, rubbing my face into the boy's belly to scent him, and then shuffled him back towards the couple standing by the front door. The man watched me with consternation, the woman with amusement, as I pushed Tay into the group of quiet children and then sat next to him. I sat patiently as he began crawling on my back, babbling nonsensically, and a few of the other children leaned towards me, petting me gently.

The hushed crowd lit up again with talk and I flinched at the sudden harshness of their voices after they had been quietly waiting, watching me. I looked to Lhiam, who was smiling at me, his eyes flickering back to Tay, who was now on my shoulders, before meeting my eyes. I couldn't read the expression in his eyes, but it took my breath away anyways. There was something... possessive in the way he watched me, and I had to snort at my own ridiculousness.

Yes, he owned me. Of course he did. But he could never belong only to me.

When Lhiam had greeted what seemed like hundreds of people, we were led inside by the couple— Melissa and Mikhal. The front door opened onto a large foyer, with a brightly blazing fire and many soft-looking arm-chairs and cushions surrounding it. Through the room they led us back to a kitchen/dining room, where there was a carved oaken table with various mismatched chairs surrounding it.

Throughout the meal, I stayed between Lhiam and Tay. The tiny boy had been set in a seat that he was strapped into, and he frequently threw food down at me, cackling when I managed to catch it in mid-air. Melissa admonished him frequently, but Lhiam's laughter at the boy's antics seemed to eventually calm her that the boy wasn't angering the prince.

Lhiam spoke with Melissa and Mikhal about Sunflower Manor through-out the meal as he passed me bits of his meat, his eyes straying to Tay, then me, multiple times throughout the meal. I wondered briefly what he was thinking as his calculating gaze watched us, as if sizing the two of us up, but I tried to force my mind not to dwell on it too long.

When the children were done eating, they were excused, leaving only Lhiam, Robert, Cain and the home's couple to finish their conversation. Without giving it much thought— Lhiam was safe enough with Robert and Cain at the table with him— I followed after Tay, who toddled into the large foyer room. When Mikhal first let him out of his little chair, the boy was covered in the gravy from the meat, and he even had a few bits of carrot in his hair. Chuffing with amusement, I cleaned him off, earning a few giggles as I ran my tongue along his face and the top of his head. He ran off after the other children, laughing in a high-pitched squeal, before I could finish, so I lumbered after him to finish cleaning him off.

16- Dream

L HIAM

Watching Edon with the boy was doing wonders to my already distracted mind. The child was loud, threw food repeatedly so that it hit Edon right in the face when he was unable to catch it in time, and he seemed to find amusement in the wolf's flustered amusement at his antics. But the wolf never once showed annoyance. He never once moved from the boy, and his attentions caused a fist to squeeze at my heart, refusing to let go. Why he seemed to have taken an affectionate shine to that boy in particular, I couldn't say.

Not to say that he ignored the other children, because from my vantage at the dining room table, I could see him chasing them around the room, obviously It in their game of Tag. The shouts of laughter almost drowned out our conversation, and Melissa made a joke about borrowing the wolf to tire the children out every night before bedtime. But the way he seemed to keep an eye on Tay, the way he forced the boy down so he could continue cleaning the food off of his face and head, and the patience he showed when the boy continuously grabbed at his tail in what I knew must be a painful hold, showed a gentle affection that had my mind racing.

Multiple images shot through my mind, all at once, and I knew then why Edon with the child was drawing my attention so closely. Images of Edon curled around Tay, napping in my bed; of the two of them playing in the south garden, Edon's laugh-filled eyes lingering on mine as he mouthed something at me; carrying Tay back to his own nursery so Edon and I could spend time alone.

Gods I wanted that. I wanted Edon; but more than that, I wanted to build a life with him. I wanted children, a family. I wanted to grow old with him, adopting as many of the country's orphans as we could possibly handle. Edon would be a wonderful, loving, nurturing father. Just watching him with the boy made me want to bring Tay home as soon as possible. Give him a home and beg Edon to share it with me.

But I shook my head at the thought. I had known the man for a little over two weeks. The thoughts were premature, and he was young. I knew he was 20 at most and may not want the same things I did. Even if he had allowed last night to happen, even if he did seem to feel some attraction for me, that didn't mean he felt for me the way I felt for him. And I couldn't force my own dreams on him and keep him from ever living the life he wanted. I couldn't tie him down, when he was just starting to live.

But gods, those images, the glimpses into a life I could only dream of, continued all the rest of the day.

When I finally got up to leave, Edon noticed immediately. He and the children were lying near the fire, soaking in its warmth as one of the older children read to the others from a large tome of stories. The four other children were sprawled around Edon, using him as a warm cushion. Two lay against his belly, another along his back. Tay was between his front paws, his face digging into Edon's neck fur as the child sucked his thumb.

The image sent a pang of want through my body that I stifled immediately. I couldn't have him; I couldn't even entertain the thoughts, or they would drive me mad. He wasn't mine, and I didn't know if he ever could be. I hoped, but I could do no more. Not yet.

But gods, the sight of him just as he looked up at me when I stood would haunt me for the rest of my life. The look in his eyes, lazy and content, the way his body was completely relaxed. It was almost better than the dreams in my head.

When he noticed me, Edon flicked his tail and gently stood, four little bodies tumbling from him, laughing as they fell. The wolf bent down to Tay, licking a gentle stripe up his cheek, before turning with a twitch of his ears and trotting over to me. When the boy realized Edon would be leaving, he cried out "doggie!" and ran at Edon, tears forming in his eyes.

Edon stomped one paw, staring down at the boy sternly, and he nudged the boy's belly, pushing him away, before turning and trotting out the door. I followed, chased out by the boy's screams. Robert laughed softly beside me as we followed the wolf, who we could tell was able to hear the child's screams long before they faded from our ears, because his big, sensitive ears kept flicking back towards the home.

I wanted to laugh with Robert, but I could almost feel Edon's distress. He hadn't wanted to leave the child. And I sympathized.

The crowds in the town were a little less dense than when we came down, since many had come out because they knew I would be in town. The early afternoon sun shone down hard, despite the chill in the air. I leaned my head back, enjoying the small bit of warmth from the sun on my face. I could feel Edon's eyes on me, but I kept my eyes closed. I had to start trying to distance myself from him, or I was going to drive myself crazy with wanting.

I was knocked from my drifting mind with a sudden flurry of motion that jerked me from my saddle. There was a sharp bark of warning, the clang of two swords being drawn, and then I was on my back ten feet from my horse, my breath knocked from me. A warm, heavy, furry body was limp on my chest, and my heart pounded as my breath returned to me in a rush. Because the body wasn't moving.

I jerked up, sliding Edon's body down into my lap, and when I saw him I wanted to scream. There was blood matted in his fur, along with two arrows, both digging into his back. He looked up at me, and I could see the pain and fear in his eyes. Luckily, he seemed to be breathing, although just barely. His breaths came in little pants for air that sounded labored. He whined, digging his nose into my palm as I stared down at him.

The commotion around me died down a bit, and then Robert was by my side.

"They're dead, sire. Three of them. Empire rogues," he whispered as he looked down at Edon with sadness. As if he was already giving up.

No. Fuck that. He would live. He wouldn't die like this. I wouldn't let him.

"Help me," I hissed, gently pulling Edon into my arms. I let Robert hold him just long enough to jump into my saddle before he let him up to me. I cradled the wolf against my chest, reveling in the warmth of his body and the way his heart beat heavily against mine.

He would live. He had to.

"You stay with me, Edon. You keep your eyes open, and you stay with me. Do you hear me?"

I kicked my stallion into motion and raced up the cobblestone path to the castle, praying to any gods, known or unknown, benevolent or otherwise, to save him.

Because as his heartbeats began to slow, I could feel my own breaking in my chest. And only knowing him a few weeks be damned. I loved him.

And I wouldn't lose him, if I had to fight the devil himself for his soul.

I whispered nonsense words of encouragement into Edon's ears as Gerard worked, gently pulling the arrows from Edon's body, cleaning the wounds, and beginning to stitch them. When I had made it to the keep's courtyard, I had leapt from my stallion, almost falling to my knees with the move, before running to Gerard's office. I screamed for the doctor, setting Edon down as gently as I could. The blood that coated my chest, arms, belly and thighs made me want to vomit, but I held myself in check as the doctor eyed me, then the wolf, and began to work without a word.

"Please, sweetheart," I whispered, my fingers digging into the fur around his neck. "Can you shift for me? The doctor needs you human so he can help you. Please, Edon."

I could feel Cain and Robert's eyes on me as I pleaded with the wolf, and their confusion was evident, but neither said a word. They had simply followed me into the room, shutting the door and all of the curious by-standers out.

Edon's wet eyes met mine, and a shudder rippled through him before his body began to twist. I barely blinked and a bloody, naked, panting, human Edon stared up at me, his eyes having never left mine. I grabbed his left hand in mine, my other hand clenching his neck to hold him steady.

"Lhiam," he whispered, and I heard a gasp and a curse of surprise from behind me.

"You're going to be alright, sweetheart," I answered, shaking my head when he tried to speak. I could feel more than see Gerard swoop in to begin to pry the arrows from Edon's body. Edon winced, but made no other move as his eyes began to drift closed.

"Let him rest," Gerard commanded from the other side of the cot. "Sleeping through the pain is the best thing for him right now."

I nodded, my entire body clenching as Edon's breaths deepened and his eyes closed almost peacefully.

I continued my fervent prayers that he would open them again.

17- Taking Hits

E DON

The first thing I noticed was the slight pressure on my side and the warmth in my hand. Someone clutched my hand gently but almost desperately, as if afraid they would hurt me. My eyes were heavy, and it took me what felt like an hour to open them. When I did, I was forced to close them again immediately, because the light was blinding and a shot of pain burst just behind my eyes.

I groaned, and the pressure in my side immediately jerked, the hand in mine squeezing.

"Edon?" Lhiam whispered huskily. I could hear the sleep in his voice and I tried to smile.

"Lhiam...?" I answered, my tongue as heavy as my eyelids seemed to be.

"Don't try to move, sweetheart," Lhiam's gruff voice sounded from just above my head. I turned towards it, my only thought to get closer to his warmth. I could hear footsteps, but Lhiam didn't move, so I wondered who else was there. Then, "Gerard is on his way back. Can you open your eyes for me?"

I opened my mouth to answer, but the words wouldn't come. Instead, I forced my eyes open, blinking rapidly to filter the light.

Lhiam stood above me, staring down at me with so much emotion in his eyes it made my heart immediately jerk against my ribs. I inhaled rapidly, studying him. There were dark shadows under his eyes, like he hadn't slept in a week. His hair stuck up haphazardly around his head, as if he had run his hands through it and hadn't bothered to fix it. I could smell that his clothes were new, and not covered in blood as I assumed they would be since he had carried me here, but despite that his shirt was ruffled, untucked, and his pants were wrinkled. As if he hadn't left my side and had been sleeping in them.

But that was a crazy thought. He had better things to do than to watch over me.

I tried to remember what had brought us here. I could remember traveling down to the group home, spending a few hours there, then the trip back. I had been distracted by Tay's cries when I heard the soft sounds of two arrows being released and felt the shift in the air as the arrows dragged towards Lhiam.

Towards Lhiam's heart.

I jumped without thought, slamming into Lhiam at the same time that two distinct jolts of pain exploded in my back. I could feel the tip of one of the arrows break off against my ribs, and my breath left me as I toppled onto Lhiam.

Then all was chaos as I felt Lhiam's arms around me, his panic, and his voice drifting over me. I let myself go, knowing he was safe, and that was all that mattered.

Now, I stared up at him, grateful he was safe, but worried about how exhausted he looked.

"Lhiam," I muttered as I felt the air behind him shift. Gerard came up behind him, immediately reaching towards my back. I lay on my belly on a soft cot. I knew I was in the doctor's offices from the sterile, too-clean smell mixed with blood around me. "Are you alright?" I managed to finish, flinching as the doctor lifted the bandages on my back, tugging at tender skin.

Lhiam glared at me, his mouth pursed as I felt a wave of disbelief and rage waft off of him. "Of course I'm alright. You jumped in front of two fucking arrows for me, Edon."

I felt my body curling away from his anger, but I fought it. I hoped it wasn't directed at me. Not really. Because how could he be angry at me doing my job? He couldn't be mad that I had done the only thing I was really good at— taking hits.

And even if his ire was directed at me, I knew he wouldn't hurt me. I tried to convince myself, and my mind understood that, but my body was far too used to that sort of rage precluding pain, so it shrank back reflexively.

"I'm sorry," Lhiam whispered when Gerard all but growled at me to hold still. "I'm sorry. Hold still, Edon. I won't hurt you. I'm not... I'm not angry. Please, calm, little wolf."

My body froze and I looked back up into Lhiam's eyes again. The sight of him still clutching my hand calmed me and I whined as he ran his hand down my cheek. I pressed my nose against his palm, scenting him. He smelled of blood, and exhaustion, and a musk that was purely Lhiam. I wanted to bury myself in his scent.

"You're healing rather quickly again," Gerard said from behind me. I kept my eyes on Lhiam, almost afraid to look away. I felt so calm, so warm, so peaceful, I dared not turn away. "There was poison in the arrows, so you're healing a bit slower than what I assume, from your past injuries, is normal for you, but the wounds are closed up and we should be able to remove the bandages soon."

I frowned, finally looking over at the doctor as he moved to stand next to Lhiam. As if hearing my unvoiced question, he smiled gently and began pulling a blanket back over my body.

"You have been out for a little less than 48 hours. It took me a few hours to get one of the arrows out of you all the way— it had managed to lodge itself in between your ribs. You're lucky. Neither was near your heart— I don't think even you would have survived that."

"Thank you," I mumbled, unsure what else to say to the man who saved my life.

"No thanks needed." He laughed, shaking his head and clapping Lhiam on the back. "You saved our prince. It was the least I could do to make sure you didn't give your life for his."

Lhiam's hand tightened in mine as he thanked Gerard, and then the doctor was gone and I was left with Lhiam. I could scent two others in the large room, and after a minute I knew who they were— Robert and Cain.

Which meant they had seen me shift.

They knew about me.

I jerked, staring around Lhiam at the men who stood guarding the door. Robert was watching me, but Cain was staring off, barely seeming aware that I existed.

"They have both sworn to keep your secret, little wolf," Lhiam said gently. He moved so he was perched on a small stool by the bedside. "They won't tell a soul."

With Lhiam's words, Cain met my eyes for a brief moment, his own eyes blank and still barely seeing me, before nodding and turning away. Robert smiled, chuckling softly as he shook his head at me.

"Yeah, kid. Your secret's safe with us."

I returned the smile hesitantly, unsure what to say in answer.

I turned back to Lhiam, the smile dropping from my lips as I met his eyes.

"Robert, Cain, can you leave us alone for a few minutes? Just wait outside the door, please."

I stiffened at Lhiam's words, flinching as I heard Robert and Cain's quiet footsteps and then the door closing.

Lhiam stood as soon as they were gone, and I fought back the whimper at the loss of his warmth on my skin.

But then my mind processed the rage he was feeling, the rage I could smell wafting from him, and my mind went blank. I watched him, wary. My body fought with the rest of me, trying to convince me to run. Hide. Fight.

But I could do none of them. I could only lay and hope he didn't leave any lasting bruises or break any bones. Broken bones could sometimes take weeks to heal.

I wondered what I had done to displease him. Was he angry that I hadn't noticed the men before I had? I should have. And if I hadn't been so distracted by little Tay, I would have. Had someone else been hurt, and he blamed me for not stopping the men sooner?

I could only guess as his rage, and then his despair rolled over me. I managed to sit up, pressing back with a wince against the wall behind me.

"Please Master," I murmured, keeping my eyes on the ground and holding my hands out to try to ward him off. But I knew there was nothing I could do to stop the blows. My pleas may only anger him further. "I'm sorry, I... I should have known they were there sooner. I..." My voice broke and I stared down at my shaking hands, horrified. I couldn't risk angering him further with my show of weakness. "I'll do better next time, Master. I pr-promise."

The silence in the room was oppressive, and I tried to fight back the wave of terror as Lhiam simply stood, completely still, staring at me. I kept my eyes from his, baring my neck, hoping my submission would calm him.

"Fucking hell," he whispered, the words cracking as he jerked back and then came towards me. I cried out, my body moving before I could stop it. I leapt from the bed, crouching on the other side from Lhiam. I wore a pair of undergarments covering my groin, but nothing else, and I shivered as the cool air touched my bare skin. The bandages strained against my back and I fought back a moan as I clutched my arms around my body.

"Edon," Lhiam croaked, frozen on the other side of the bed. He stared down at me, his eyes huge in a face filled with shock and horror. "Sweetheart, please," he began, but then his eyes fluttered and he was falling.

I jumped forward, scrambling to Lhiam's side as his knees hit the floor with a harsh sounding crack. I pushed past my own fear, praying he wouldn't lash out, as I reached him. I studied him, taking in his scent, his pale skin, his labored breaths, and realized his knees had given out on him in exhaustion.

I could smell it wafting off of him. He was past innervation. And I couldn't even scent when the last time he ate was.

"M-master?" I asked, reaching a hand out to offer to help him to his feet. He sat back on his ass, pulling away from my hand, slumping down and leaning his head against the cot behind him.

"Stop calling me that," he growled, glaring up at me. But the rage that had permeated from him was dying down, leaving only shame and horror. "My name is Lhiam. I am not your master, Edon. You don't fucking belong to anyone, do you hear me?"

I sat back on my heels and shook my head, confused. He had been so angry, but now he was only watching me, as if I had done something to hurt him.

"Yes, Lhiam," I answered.

"I'm not angry with you, Edon," he continued, shaking his head as he dropped his eyes. "I'm angry at the men who almost killed you. I'm angry that I put you in the position you were in, the one where you felt the need to jump in front of those arrows. You shouldn't have. They were meant for me. I'm angry that I wasn't able to protect you. And now I'm devastated that I caused you to be so afraid of me that you—"

His voice broke off, cracking painfully, and I leaned forward, afraid I might miss his next words.

"I was so scared, Edon," he whispered, his entire body shaking as tears slipped down his cheeks. I stared, stunned, as he gruffly rubbed at the tears, as if annoyed they had fallen. "I thought I had lost you. I thought I wouldn't get another chance..." He shook his head, biting his lip to cut off his own words, and then finally turned up to stare into my eyes. "Please don't ever do that again, Edon. I don't want to live without you."

18- Healing

L HIAM

I had never felt joy and relief like I did when Edon groaned and then opened his eyes, staring up at me. Two days— two fucking days— of staring down at him, holding his hand, sleeping only minutes at a time, my head pillowed against the cot at his side. I feared I would never see those amber eyes again. That I would never see that soft smile, those hesitant laughs, that beautiful body moving with grace.

And then he was awake, and I was floating. Until I remembered why he was in that bed in the first place. Why he had almost bled out.

For me. Because he was putting his body in danger to protect my life.

It couldn't happen again. And if I had to lock him up in my bedchambers for the rest of his life, I would. He couldn't be hurt again. Not for me. I couldn't be the reason his beautiful life was cut short.

I sent out Robert and Cain, ready to try to find a solution. I would find Edon another job. He could stay by Lacy's side, but neither of them were allowed to go outside the keep walls anymore. I couldn't risk either of them. I would find him another occupation if he wanted. He could train as a healer under Gerard, or work in the gardens, the library, anything that kept him away from danger.

My rage at the men who had tried to kill me, and who had almost succeeded in tearing open my heart by taking my wolf from me, was heady, but I tried to push it away. They had paid with their lives, and I had to be satisfied with that. Even though I wished they had lived so that I could make their deaths long and unbearably painful.

When I was quiet too long, trying to sort through my thoughts, I turned to Edon, ready to explain. Ready to beg him to stay with me, to try to feel for me what I felt for him.

And then his words tumbled out of him in a rushed, devastated jumble, and I wanted to be sick. He was pleading with me not to hurt him, and my confusion was short lived as I realized that he must sense my emotions as well as any animal could, and then I felt only shame. Shame and horror as he continued to beg me, holding back, as if he knew nothing he said would really stop me from hurting him.

How could he possibly think I was angry at him? After what he had done for me?

But the answer was obvious. He felt my rage, thought it was directed at him, and everything he had ever encountered told him that when a man with power over him was angry, they would take it out on him. On his flesh, drawing blood.

"Fucking hell," I gasped, feeling bile rise in my throat.

When he leapt from the bed to get away from me, I felt my knees give out on me. I knew I was pushing myself the last two days, but I hadn't been able to eat or sleep while Edon's life hung in the balance. I had tried to eat the venison stew Robert brought me a few hours after Gerard had finished with Edon, along with a change of clothes for me, and I had ended up retching up the three bites I had managed to force down. The little sleep I had gotten had been disturbed each time Edon's breathing changed, or any part of his body twitched or moved.

When he hesitantly called me master again, I thought my heart was going to break. I grimaced, clutching at my chest. But when I finally managed to get out almost everything my heart was screaming at him, keeping back my overwhelming love for him, because I feared that he would either be scared away by it, or worse, that he would feel indebted to fake the affection back, he was still.

He watched me for a few moments, simply observing as the horridly embarrassing tears poured down my face. Then his fingers were brushing at my cheeks, rubbing the tears away, and he was bringing his wet fingers to his lips. He licked them, his eyes never leaving mine. He leaned towards me, and then he was crawling into my lap. I spread my legs, giving him room, and soon he was curled up against my chest, his head resting on my shoulder, his hot breaths painting shudders across my neck.

"I'm sorry, Lhiam," he whispered, and I bit back a groan. His words were said almost directly against my ear, the vibrations and his hot breath sending jolts down my spine. "I don't know... I don't know why I was so afraid. I know you wouldn't hurt me, I just... For a moment, I was back there, with them, and I..."

I nodded, wrapping my arms around him as gently as I could. I dug my nose into his hair, taking a deep breath in. He smelled like herbs, wolf, and a scent that was uniquely Edon, and the smells had my dick twitching, although I knew in the state I was in, it wouldn't do anything more than perk up in interest. And if it did, it would be sorely disappointed.

"I understand. I'm sorry I was so angry. I should have known it would scare you. I wasn't thinking. I haven't been getting a lot of sleep." I tried to feign laughter, but it came out as a pathetic, almost mewling sound.

He shook his head against my neck, and I felt his lips press against my pulse point for just a moment.

"You are nothing like them, and I am ashamed I thought you were, even if only for a few moments."

I shuddered in horror but nodded. "Thank you, little wolf."

We lay in each other's arms for a few more minutes before Edon pulled away from me, helped me to my feet, lay back on the cot, and dragged me down with him. That was how Gerard found us an hour later— Edon breathing softly in my arms, his head resting against my chest as I clutched him tightly to my body, our legs entwined like a braid. Feeling him safe, warm, and his heart beating next to mine did wonders for my exhaustion, and I managed to sleep until Gerard woke me with a hand on my arm.

"I'm going to remove the bandages, and then you can take him to his room, Your Highness. I'll come visit him a few more times, but he's healed remarkably. Again."

Edon woke with a sleepy whimper, and soon Gerard had deemed him healthy enough to be on his own, and I was carrying him back to the sleeping chambers. But rather than taking him to his room, I dragged him to mine. Gerard and I had dressed him in a simple pair of cotton breeches and shirt, and I held him tight against my chest, wrapped up in a blanket, but I could still feel him shivering against me.

As I moved through the halls, backed by Robert and Cain, who had been part of my vigil since Edon had been injured, but who had both managed to swap out sleeping a few hours at a time, and both had managed to eat what was brought to them from the kitchens, I could feel the many sets of eyes watching me. Most were simply curious, but a few were angry at my obvious display of affection and special attention for an unknown man.

Despite the law being on my side, many in my country, and beyond, would still see my love as an abomination, a crime against the gods, against nature.

They could go fuck themselves.

I laid Edon down on my large bed, ensuring he had enough blankets covering him, before I called for a meal and for my fire to be stoked. The room was freezing, since it had been two days since I had stepped foot inside it. My orders were quickly followed, and soon both Edon and I had managed to choke down a bowl of broth each, and both lay back under the covers, holding each other again.

19- Just Feel

EDON

Over the next two days, Lhiam's tender care knew no bounds. By the time I woke after arriving in his room, I was almost completely back to full strength, but he either didn't believe me, or he just didn't want to leave the bed, because he refused to let me go.

We ate our meals— light soups, breads, and then eventually sandwiches and hearty slabs of meat— in the bed, and then we slept curled up around each other. I woke a few times to Lhiam rubbing a medicinal salve over my back, and I fell back to sleep as his fingers worked into my skin. We woke only to eat, and I noticed our meals were only brought in by either Robert or Cain. No one else entered the room, and I wondered if that was to keep Lhiam's dirty secret of sleeping with me, or if it was something else.

Gods, I prayed it was something else, but my simple mind couldn't come up with another reason why only the two men would be allowed to see the two of us together.

My fear when I had first woken shamed me. Lhiam had been so good to me, so kind, and he had never raised a hand in anger toward me, and yet I had treated him like the monster my masters had been.

My mind had simply blanked, and my "training" had taken over. Every time my masters had beaten or raped me into submission had rushed through my mind, and I had been unable to think past the anger Lhiam was unconsciously projecting and the answering terror that wrapped my body in its cocoon of self-preservation.

My mind knew that Lhiam wouldn't hurt me. It knew that Lhiam had promised me he would never touch me unless I wanted him to. And it believed him. But the rest of me sneered, shocked that I could be so naive as to believe a man. A human.

I hoped Lhiam would prove that other voice in my mind wrong. But for now, I could only trust him, because my body craved him, and my heart ached for him to be true, and for his words to be genuine. And with each gentle action he took to care for me, my hope grew.

I bathed the first time I woke fully in Lhiam's chambers, washing the bits of blood from my body that Gerard hadn't been able to get off when he had cleaned me. And just as he had the first night I was in the keep, Lhiam washed my body while I sat watching him. Although there was a definite difference between then and now.

The first time I had bathed in this stone building, that night that felt like a lifetime before, I had been terrified. My body had been torn up by Master, my soul had been afraid to breathe, and my body had jerked each time Lhiam's fingers brushed against me.

Now, I leaned into his touch. I craved it. My injuries were healed almost completely, leaving behind only a few raised, tender spots, but Lhiam brushed over me as if I was made of glass. I tried to tell him I could wash myself, blushing heavily at his attentions. As a wolf, and especially as a man who had spent much of my life naked in front of others, I wasn't modest or embarrassed by being naked, but his hands on my skin felt like fire and I could feel my cock harden. And for that I was ashamed.

"Lhiam," I whined, pulling away from him and yet leaning towards him at the same time, as he brought the cloth down my stomach toward where I wanted him the most. I leaned back reflexively to give him room as my hips jerked up against his hand, my cock seeking friction. I felt him pause, and then he huffed out in amusement and he was rubbing the cloth up my inner thighs.

"No, not—" I began, but I broke off when he gently gripped my balls to wash them with the cloth.

I moaned, turning my head and burying my face in his fully clothed shoulder. I didn't know when he had managed to bathe, but I knew from his scent that he had sometime after we had come to his room.

"It's ok, little wolf," he said gently, his voice gravelly against my ear. "Let go. I've got you. Always."

I cried out as, in one fluid motion, he moved behind me, his arms wrapping around me. One hand gripped my cock firmly while the other continued to fondle my balls. I jerked up, humping into his palm as I reached back, my fingers entwining in his shirt, my face and wet head digging into his chest.

"Shhh," he groaned as my pants began to echo around the large chamber. "Hold still and just feel, sweetheart."

I tried to calm my jerking hips, and was fairly successful, with only a few sporadic shudders I couldn't quite hold back. Lhiam began to drag his hand up and down, slowly and sensually at first. He gently stroked my balls at the same time, and I saw stars as I clenched my eyes shut, biting his shirt to keep from crying out.

His right hand around my cock began to speed up as he released my balls. I sobbed in complaint at the release in pressure, but soon stiffened as his fingers smoothly stroked down my taint, his destination unmistakable.

"Tell me no and I stop now, sweetheart," he said against my head, his face buried in the hair near my ear. A spasm wracked my body as his breathy words hit the sensitive skin of my ears. "I can make you come without fingering your anus."

"No... Don't stop. Please. Want you inside me," I answered, only hoping my words had come out understandably, rather than the nonsensical jumble that hit my ears. I spread my legs, gasping as I felt the water tease my ass. "Don't stop. Please don't stop."

Lhiam's grunt and the shudder that ran through his body was the only answer I got as his fingers continued to stroke down my taint. When he pressed one finger against my hole, I thought my body would jump from the tub. I jerked, crying out as my back arched. Lightning lit my spine, and Lhiam groaned in my ear.

"Gods, you're so fucking responsive, little wolf," he hissed, and then he was rubbing and fingering my pucker and I lost all sense of anything else but his fingers on my hole, his fist clutching my cock up and down, up and down, and his breaths in my ear as I whimpered nonsensically against his chest.

When I felt my pleasure peak, when my balls drew up, ready to spurt into the water sloshing violently around me, and I was sobbing that I was so close, so close, Lhiam pulled away completely. I cried out, growling in frustration as I was yanked back from the edge.

"Not yet. Not yet, beautiful," Lhiam grunted, and then his hands were back on me. But the fingers at my hole no longer simply poked and rubbed against me. One finger breached me, and I stiffened at the stretch. But it wasn't unpleasant and there was no pain, only a slight burn that made tingles dance up my spine. His hand on my cock was again slow, steady, drawing gasps from me when he twisted his wrist when he reached the head, rubbing his calloused palm over the tip, before dragging it back down my shaft.

The finger inside me began to explore, rubbing against my inner walls, and I moaned at the unfamiliar sensations running through my body. There were plenty of men who had taken their pleasure inside my body, but none had taken the time to prepare me like this. None had done anything more than thrust their hard cocks into my body until their own completion. Even the ones who got off on seeing me come had only pounded into me, yanking on my cock painfully until I came with a sob of pleasured agony.

No, this was all new. This was all uniquely Lhiam, and I treasured his perusal of my body. It was his, until he grew tired of it. Just as I was his until he grew tired of me and threw me away. So until then I would give him everything, and I would accept anything he chose to give me in return.

Like this pleasure, in this moment.

When his finger inside of me touched something that sent heat up my spine and had my cock leaking into the water, I cried out. He rubbed it again and I bit into his shoulder, drawing a hiss from him, along with a chuckle.

"Gods but I love your teeth on me," he growled. I wanted to answer, to tell him that I loved everything he was doing, that I needed him to never let me go, but my mind wouldn't focus and soon I was on the edge again.

"Please don't stop, Lhiam," I managed, my hands reaching up to gently caress his neck as I continued to press my face against his chest. My body was twisted at an awkward angle— my back to him, my legs spread wide in the tub, my face smashed against his chest, but I didn't care. There was only one thing my mind could think of : release. "Please. Need it— you. Need to—"

I couldn't force the words out, but Lhiam seemed to understand. Like he always seemed to somehow understand the words I couldn't quite voice. He sped up his hand, his finger inside me pressing up hard against that magical spot. I felt my building ecstacy burst and I screamed, my body jerking violently in the water. I lost all sense of everything but the agony ripping down my spine as he stroked me through the violent orgasm, my cum releasing into the water. My balls released everything inside of them, and when I finally managed to come back down, Lhiam was gently stroking me through the aftershocks.

He gradually pulled his finger out of my hole, and then he was helping me to stand, wrapping a warm towel around my body, and lifting me from the tub.

Lhiam simply held me in his arms, his soaked clothes rubbing against my damp towel. I could feel his erection press against my belly, but I could do nothing about it. It was at least a few minutes before my breathing had calmed enough that I could pull myself away from Lhiam and stare up at him.

He smiled down at me, and then his lips were on mine and I was lost again.

20- Have To Know

***** *So, so much trigger warning***

LHIAM

Watching Edon writhe beneath me in the bath was everything I had needed. To see him so alive, feeling so much pleasure, was like a balm on my still-fractured nerves. When he tipped over, screaming against my chest, his body lifting from the water as he broke apart, I couldn't help the satisfied smile that lit my face.

I helped him from the bath, his legs shaking and barely holding his weight, and simply held him. I soaked up his scent, the feel of his warm breaths on my neck as he rose up on his toes to be nearer to me, and the shudders that slowly calmed as his breathing evened out and his heartbeat slowed.

When his pleasure-dazed eyes, dark with barely-contained lust, stared into mine, I swooped down and devoured his mouth, thrusting my tongue in to the sounds of his low growls. He grabbed my hair, holding me against him, and a shot of pleasure down my spine generated from that contact.

"Lhiam," he groaned as he pulled away, his eyes still closed. "Please. I want you inside of me."

I fought everything inside me that wanted to trip him to the ground and rut inside of him until I found my release. The animal part of myself that wanted to bury myself inside of him and never let him leave my bed.

Mine.

But the sensible, sane bit of my mind rebelled. Not only could I never hurt him, but I needed to make this perfect for him. I needed to wipe out everything terrible from his past and replace it with what I made him feel. Replace it with me.

And if that was selfish, then so be it.

"I know, little wolf," I whispered, pulling his thrusting body from mine. As if he knew my thoughts had begun to straighten, the young man had begun rubbing his semi-erect cock against my pants. And his little hitches in breath were threatening to take all sense of thought from my mind again. "But not yet. We need to talk first."

"Talk later," he pouted, trying to break free of the iron grip I had on his hips, holding his body from mine.

"No. Talk now," I answered stubbornly, drawing a growl from him that sounded eerily like his wolf. "I've told you before, Edon. I won't be another thing that keeps you awake at night. So before we can do anything more, I need a few answers."

He stiffened against me, shame marking his cheeks dark, and then backed away. I could visibly see his cock softening beneath the towel, and a small part of me cursed my idiocy.

But then I looked into his pain-darkened eyes and I knew I had made the right decision. Until I knew more, I couldn't possibly take advantage of him. I had to know how deep his scars went, at least so I was aware. So I could help him fight his demons if they cropped up while I was inside of him.

We dressed quickly, Edon donning a shirt for the first time since he had entered my room. We had mostly kept him naked from the waist up so it was easier for me to rub Gerard's salve into his back. I changed out of my wet clothes and into a comfortable shirt and leggings, and then we sat on the bed.

To my joy, Edon waited until I was sitting back against the headboard before he crawled up and into my arms. I wrapped them around him, holding his back against my chest, twining our legs together before dragging the blankets up over us. Edon pressed back against me, and I flinched when his ass rubbed up against my still-throbbing cock.

When he seemed to be settled, and as relaxed as he was going to be, I began. "Edon, can you tell me about your past?"

"What do you want to know, Lhiam?" he asked, his voice so quiet I wouldn't have heard him if he wasn't inches from my ears.

"Everything. I want to know anything you're willing to tell me. Start at the beginning, and if you need a break, we can do that."

"Why, Lhiam?" Edon finally gasped out, after what felt like an eternity in silence. "Why do you need to know? Do you want to know how many men have fucked me? Because I don't have the answer to that. I can take a guess, but the number makes me want to vomit, so I'm not sure how you'll be able to look at me after.

"Do you want to know that my Master preferred to use his hooked cat o' nine tails over his belt, because it made me scream louder? Do you want to hear about how he would try to make me scar by rubbing mud in the wounds to keep them open longer, because I healed too godsdammed fast for his liking? That my first Master, because I've had two, you see, didn't even wait for me to hit puberty before he was splitting me open on his cock? Is that what you want to know?"

I could feel the sob trying to reach its way out of my chest but I held it back. He needed me to be strong for him. His voice was so dead, so devoid of emotion, like he was talking about the weather or a conversation he overheard rather than something that made me want to scream until my vocal chords bled.

"I don't want to know. Gods Edon, I don't want to know. If I could spend the rest of my life never hearing about the horrors you've been subjected to I'd die a very happy man. But I have to know. Because I need to know you, Edon, and the things you've been through are a part of you. Not a prominent part, because you are not your scars, but they are your past. They're your fears and they helped shape you into the beautiful, kind, patient, selfless, and awe-inspiring man I've come to know."

His shaking sobs against my chest sounded as if they were ripped from the very depths of his soul. He turned his body, twisting up the blankets around us, so he could shove his face against my chest.

"I don't want to know, Edon," I repeated, shaking my head as I stroked my hands up and down his back. His sobs were almost violent, shaking him and forcing his entire body limp against me. "But I need to know you. Please share yourself with me. As much as you can bear. I can take it. And I think you need to share it. We can carry it together, now. You're not alone. Not anymore."

Edon's sobs slowed after a few minutes, and he fell lax against me, hiccuping with every inhale. It was over twenty minutes before he finally spoke, his voice deeper, almost a void. I wanted to cringe from that voice, but I held him tight as he fingered a loose strand from my shirt.

"My Ma and Pa were poor. I don't... really remember them much. I don't even remember what country or realm we lived in. Only that we lived in a small cottage in the woods. My Pa was big, although I was small even when I was a pup, so maybe he wasn't so big and that was just how I saw him..." Edon paused, as if gathering his thoughts, before continuing.

"We were poor, but we were happy. I remember my Pa kissing my Ma a lot. I used to laugh and wrinkle my nose, but I liked seeing them together. There was something... warm about it.

"The first time I shifted to a wolf, I was three at most. My Ma panicked, thinking I had run off, but I shifted back in front of her and she understood. When she told my Pa, he was angry at first, thinking she was telling a bad joke. But then I did it again, and he knew. I was a freak.

"My memory gets kind of... fuzzy. I don't remember much. I remember we were happy, my parents tried to keep my secret, because they knew others wouldn't understand, and I remember laughter. So much laughter and joy and love...

"And then there was only blood and fire and I was running. My Ma was screaming at me to run, to escape. I don't know who killed them. I don't know why. But I suspect it was my fault, because I remember the anger in the eyes of the men. The anger and the hatred and I didn't understand why they hated me so much.

"I wandered for what felt like forever before I came upon a mountain pack. They adopted me in, although they thought me strange. I spent most of the next few years as a wolf. I forgot how to speak. I forgot about my Ma and Pa. I was only a wolf, with an alpha and a pack, and I was content.

"Every once in awhile, as if my body got tired of being one shape, I would shift back to human against my will. It was one of those times that my first master found me. I don't know his name. I probably heard it at some point, but I only ever called him Master."

"How..." I cut in, swallowing deeply before clutching Edon tighter to my chest and shaking my head. "How old were you?"

"I think I was 5 when my Ma and Pa died, and then 8 when Master found me. I'm not sure, because wolves don't really celebrate birthdays, of course, or mark time, really, but the timing... feels right, I suppose."

I nodded, biting back an agonized growl. He was a child. He was a baby, and some man had ripped his childhood and innocence from him, after he had already had his entire world torn to shreds around him.

It took Edon a few more minutes to compose himself after my interruption. I waited as patiently as I could, rubbing my hand up and down his back as he breathed deeply in and out, his nose pressed against my chest. When he finally seemed ready again, he pulled away, putting his back to my front again and sighing as he relaxed against me. He was still tense, his legs twitching around mine, but I only tightened my grip on him all the more.

"I was drinking from a stream in my human form when my Master came up. He talked to me sweetly, told me he had dinner for me if I wanted— I was probably half starved. It was the middle of winter. I followed after him, because I remembered the food humans had. Cooked meat, goat's milk— I was practically drooling. He led me to his camp, tied me up, and I never saw my pack again.

"I was with him for a few years. I think maybe 4 or 5, because I got too old for him, and he always said anyone above the age of 11 wasn't 'tight enough'. He traveled around. I don't know what he did for work, but he always seemed to have enough to eat, and if we were visiting a town or city, we stayed in inns. But he didn't have a permanent home. We were always travelling. He would tell the innkeepers I was his son, or his nephew, or his brother. I went along with it, because I knew the punishment if I didn't. I tried to escape a few times, and each time he managed to catch me. And make me regret it."

His shiver told me that the punishment was severe enough for him to still feel the echoes of the agony, even now, all these years later.

"When I got to be too old, he sold me to a carnival performer, who used me in his act. My second Master never fucked me. I don't think he was attracted to boys, because I saw him with plenty of women and young girls over the years, but he did like to hurt me. And he could be... creative. When he would get an interested party, or he ran low on money, or I didn't make enough in the show, he would sell my body to men willing to pay. He would..."

With his pause, I could all but feel the growl that wanted to rip from Edon's throat. I dug my face into his hair, my hands soothing up and down his arms and chest as I held him to me.

"I don't know..." he choked, shaking his head. I couldn't see his face, but I knew his eyes were clenched with barely withheld tears. "I don't know how much of me is wolf, and how much is man. I don't even know why I am both. But I know there are things about me that I can attribute to the lupine side of me. I don't like enclosed spaces. It's more than being in the cage so long; it's instinctive. I don't like walls, and being locked up. And Master learned that early. He also learned that my human teeth can break skin just as easily as my wolf fangs. So after the first few men complained about me fighting them, he...he got a muzzle he would put on me, when he would sell me. But that just made me panic and fight harder, so he began to tie me to the bed. It got to the point where he would pull me from the cage after the showing, tie me spread eagle on my face on the bed, with the muzzle on, and charge... admission into the cart. They each usually had 30 minutes, and they had to pay extra if more than one wanted to go at the same time, because that meant I might be too injured for more men for the rest of the night—"

I gasped out a sob, no longer able to hold back the tears. My body was wracked with sobs as I leaned over, wrapping my arms around him so tightly he was smashed against me in what I knew had to be an uncomfortable embrace. I wrapped my legs around his, drawing them in, and simply held him that way. I could feel a few hot tears hit my arms from him, but he was all but silent as I tried to rein in my fury, my agony, and my horror. I hadn't ever guessed... I had known he had been hurt, had known that he likely had been raped, but I could never have imagined this. It was too much.

Edon was quiet for so long, I wondered if he had fallen to sleep. His breaths were even, his heartbeat slow and steady. My own sobs had died down and were only hiccups against his neck when he finally spoke again.

"If you changed your mind, I can go," he whispered, his voice cracking as I stiffened against him. "I understand. I'm a whore, and I'm... I'm dirty. It would be better for you, easier, if you were to find someone else to warm your bed who—"

His words were cut off by me jumping from the bed. I barely made it to the chamber pot before I spewed up everything in my stomach. His harsh sob behind me was the only thing that made it past the roaring sound in my ears.

21- Broken

EDON

With each word, I felt myself digging my own grave. How could he ever want to fuck me now? Now that he knew I was used, dirty, broken? He would throw me away now, and I knew that with confidence with each word. But it was like vomit— once I started I couldn't stop. I couldn't halt the words spewing from my mouth, describing the disgusting way I had lived my entire life.

And then he was leaping from the bed to get away from me, to throw up in the chamber pot, and the earth shattered beneath me.

I couldn't breathe. I couldn't see anymore. I couldn't hear anything past his hacking into the pot. I had to escape. I couldn't stay there anymore. I couldn't bear to see his look of disgust, his words demanding I leave and never return. His horror when he remembered how he had touched me, kissed me, almost been inside of me.

Dirty. Used. Disgusting.

I gasped in a few breaths, leaping from the bed. My only thought was escape, but I couldn't shift. My heart shattering in my chest was too much for my wolf, and he was hiding deep in my mind. Even when I tried to call for him, he only whined in return.

I slammed against the door, scrabbling for the doorknob, when I heard him call my name. I cried out, yanking the door open before he was able to reach for me. I had thought he wouldn't hurt me, but he was so angry at me for allowing him to touch me when I knew how dirty I was, I feared he wanted to make sure I knew I had made a mistake. He would punish me for daring to believe that he could want me. For daring to believe I was anything more than a whore, filth, trash. Everything Master had ever called me.

I almost tripped on Robert, who stared at me as if I had grown a second head. I held back another sob as Lhiam called my name again. And then he was yelling for Robert, and the guard was reaching for me, and I screamed out in defiance and leapt back. I still couldn't shift, but my human legs would just have to do.

I ran down the hall at a full sprint, but a heavy force slammed into me before I had managed a dozen steps, knocking my breath from me as Lhiam's scent hit my nostrils. He yanked my hands up, pressing them to the wall above me with only one of his big palms, caging me in with his body. He glared down at me, fury in his eyes. Fury and desperation and agony.

"Please, Master," I sobbed, shaking my head and trying to escape his hold. But he held me so tightly I flinched at his heavy hands. "Please, let me go. I'll go. You don't have to... Please, I'm sorry. I'm sorry I'm sorry I'm sorry..." I continued, but Lhiam only began to drag me back to his room with both of my wrists encircled in one of his big hands.

"Leave now, Robert," he commanded, and then the door was shutting behind him, Robert's concerned eyes watching me just as the door closed him out.

Lhiam let me fall to the ground, releasing me with a sigh. I crumpled, curling around myself, trying to make as small a target as I could.

"Look at me, Edon," he whispered. I froze as my mind began to clear. His hands on my face dragged me up until I was forced to stare into his eyes. "I can't control the anger or the disgust you feel from me, Edon, but I can tell you it is not directed at you. Please look into my eyes, sweetheart. I'm sorry. I'm so, so sorry that I scared you again. Please, sweetheart. Please don't leave me."

I forced my eyes to meet his, and what I saw had me drawing back in confusion. He looked pained. Like I had hurt him somehow. I cast my mind back, trying to remember if I had lashed out and hit him, but my panicked state had left my mind empty except for the need to escape, so I could barely remember having run in the first place.

Why couldn't I stop hurting him?

"What you said, about being... about being dirty. Being a whore. When you said it, I heard it in their voices. I wasn't hearing you, I was hearing them. And I couldn't stop from being sick. I do not think you are dirty. I think you are loving and kind and a hundred other beautiful things. Dirty is not a descriptor that could ever be used to describe you."

I shook my head, unsure what he wanted from me. Just because he was being kind about what he had heard changed nothing. There was no way he could still want me. Not after everything I had told him— everything I had done to other men. That I had let them do to me so the pain would stop.

"I think we should talk about some things," he whispered, and I knew. He was going to get rid of me. He was so kind, he wouldn't beat me. He wouldn't be angry at me for lying. But I couldn't stay. And I especially couldn't stay with him the way we had been. He must be so disgusted just touching me now.

"Please Lhiam," I gasped, daring to clutch at his tunic with frantic fingers. "Please let me stay. I want to be here. Near you. I don't want to leave. Please, Lhiam. I understand that you don't want to fuck me anymore, not with everything I told you, but let me stay. I won't ever come near you as a human. I will stay a wolf all the time; I just want to be here with you."

"Edon, I don't think you could possibly understand what I'm feeling right now. For the second time in a matter of days, the man I'm falling in love with has gone into a full panic, terrified I was going to hurt him. And now he's telling me he'll never let me see his exquisite body or his stunning soul again.

"Why do you think I'm going to send you away? Love, how could I possibly send away my heart? How could I force you to leave, when you would be taking the other half of my heart and soul with you?"

Lhiam paused, shaking his head as he stood and moved away from me. I stared up at him, dumbfounded. Had I heard him right? No, it wasn't possible. I was a plaything. A bed warmer for him to pleasure himself, but only for a time. Until he found someone else, another toy, or he married a woman with royal blood. Then I would be forgotten.

So why would he say those things? Why was he being so cruel? He could have my body anytime, even if I didn't desire it. Why was he demanding my heart and soul as well?

"Edon, you are always free to go. I'll never hold you prisoner. I stopped you from running just now because I feared you would hurt yourself in your panic to escape, but I will never keep you against your will. If you want to go, you are free to. But know that I don't want you to go. And I'll even go so far as to beg. Stay with me, my love." He turned to me, and his eyes were dark, agonized, and wet with unshed tears. "Please don't leave me. I love you. I love you so much, little wolf."

22- Choice

✱ *smuttiness ahead :):) (I'm such a perv)**

LHIAM

The minute the words left my mouth, I regretted them. Because Edon's eyes shuttered, and I could almost feel the disbelief rolling off of him. I wanted to cry out at him to stop letting them hurt him. I wanted to track down every man who had ever hurt him, made him feel dirty; made him feel so worthless that he couldn't believe that someone could love him.

But with the regret came the relief. I had been holding the emotions in for what felt like an eternity, and I had finally let go.

And if I had to spend the rest of my life proving it to him, I would.

But he had to give me the chance.

I couldn't force him to stay.

"Lhiam," he began hesitantly, and I counted it as a victory that he hadn't called me Master. I held my hand up, stopping him before he could break my heart.

"It's alright, little wolf. I understand your hesitation. I honestly had no intention of telling you of my feelings, because I don't want to hold you down in any way, and that counts keeping you prisoner with my feelings. Just know I don't want you to leave, alright? Will you stay with me?"

His nod was instantaneous, and I smiled with relief. "I'm glad," I whispered. "Now, if it's alright, I'd like to wash out my mouth. I'll be right back."

When I returned from the changing room Edon was still in the same place. He stared down at his bare feet, his face calculating.

"If you want to return to your room, you're welcome—"

"I want to stay here with you, Lhiam," he answered, and I couldn't help but feel pride at the confidence in his tone. "If that pleases you."

"Spending time with you always pleases me, little wolf," I answered with a somewhat forced grin. His tiny return smile set my heart aflame, especially when he looked up and met my eyes.

"I'm glad."

Edon held out his hand with a heavy blush and I pushed myself into his arms, taking a deep breath of his scent. "I'm sorry I hurt you again, little wolf. I don't mean to, but you sensing my emotions is a bit... problematic."

I could feel him huff in amusement against my chest. "It is," he said simply. "I'm sorry I panicked again, Lhiam. I don't know—"

"— Little wolf, you never have to apologize to me for feeling fear. I only wish there was some way for me to take it from you. I would in a moment, if I could."

"I know," he answered, almost as if he was surprised by the admission. "I know you would."

Edon pulled away from me, looking up into my eyes, and I jerked when I felt his cock nudging up against my stomach. I had been amazed, when he was telling me his story, that he had ever allowed me to touch him, much less felt such pleasure at my touch. So now I was shocked anew that he could desire someone, after everything he had been through. Everything evil men had made him endure.

"Lhiam," he whined, jerking when I pulled his hips up flush against my body. "I want you."

I shook my head, unsure if I should push him. I didn't know if I should take advantage of him, after everything he had been through. How could he possibly want to be with me, after everything that had just happened, everything I had put him through?

"Please, Lhiam. I want you. I want you to show me how it's supposed to be." He paused, looking up to meet my eyes. "I've never wanted like this before. Never desired another. But with you, I can barely breathe when you're near. I want to know what it feels like to..."

"Gods I want to make love to you, little wolf," I whispered, leaning down so my lips were just barely brushing his. "I need to know that you will stop if you feel even slightly uncomfortable. I need you to promise me, Edon. You tell me no, and I will stop, no questions asked."

"Yes, Lhiam," he answered, his blush deepening as I studied his face.

I nodded and dragged him up for a kiss, then led him back to the bed. He began to yank on his shirt, his fingers visibly shaking. I grabbed his hands, dipping down to slant my mouth over his. He melted against me as I made love to his mouth, his shaking subsiding until he was breathing deeply but calmly in my arms. I pulled away, slowly lifting his shirt above his head. A few deep scars marred his back, and the puckered scars from the recent arrows were fading alongside them, but otherwise he was completely clear of blemish. I wondered for a moment how many scars would show if he didn't heal as quickly and wholly as he did.

I banished the thought as quickly as it came. I couldn't make this perfect for him if I couldn't pull my mind from the past. And this had to be perfect for him. Because if the gods were willing to gift me with him, I would spend the rest of my life making love to him, and this would only be the first time we joined our bodies. The gods willing, this was the first step to the rest of our lives together.

But it had to be perfect. I couldn't hurt him, and I couldn't let him feel anything less than overwhelming ecstasy. Because my perfect man deserved nothing less than everything.

I removed my own shirt, then his pants, letting them fall to the ground around his ankles. His blush rose up to his ears now, and I wanted to laugh. Never before had he been embarrassed about his nakedness; he barely seemed to notice it, usually. But now he watched me like a virgin on his wedding night, and the look made my cock harden so quickly in my pants I almost fell over from dizziness.

Because that's what he was— a virgin. Because none of those other men meant anything. They were nothing, and he was everything. He had never chosen them.

He chose me.

When I pulled my own pants down, letting my hard cock free, he took in a deep breath. His eyes rolled over my cock, balls, and then back up to meet my eyes. His smile was small, but there was no hesitation or fear on his face. Only excitement and nervousness. I gently dragged his undergarments down, freeing his cock, and stared when I saw it clearly for the first time. I had gripped it in my hands, had felt it rubbing against my own cock and against my belly, but I had never really looked at it. It was shorter than mine but thicker, and the base, just above his balls, had a ridge, almost a protrusion.

I had never seen anything like it, but it was titillating and had me wondering how it would feel against the rim of my ass as he pounded into me.

I shuddered at the thought before dragging my eyes away and pulling Edon back. After pulling a bottle of oil from the drawer beside my bed out and setting it down near the pillows, I laid back on the bed, pulling Edon up onto me, and watched him get acclimated to the new position. After hearing about how he was always tied up face down on the bed, I knew I couldn't loom over him. Especially this first time. I had to make sure he knew he was in control.

My head resting against the headboard, I watched as Edon sat up, straddling my hips, his cock jutting out proudly. He rocked his hips once, twice, and then growled down at me. Ordering me to hurry up.

I reached up, running both hands up and down Edon's thin chest and stomach. He had filled out since he had come to live in the castle, his ribs no longer visible through thin skin, but he was still skinny, his belly dipping as I pressed a finger into the belly button at the center. He chuckled breathlessly, then leaned down, putting his chest within reaching distance of my mouth. I took advantage, reaching up and running a thick swipe of my tongue over one of his nipples. He moaned, pushing his fingers through my hair to hold me to him. I scooted my body down a bit, then guided him up so he was straddling my shoulders. He watched me, following my moves, and when his cock rested against my lips and I opened my mouth, he gasped.

"Lhiam," Edon began, as if to protest, but I ignored him, taking the head in and swirling and poking my tongue along the tip. His gasp was immediate, and the way he arched his back, thrusting his hips mindlessly had his cock spearing to the back of my throat. I reached my hands back, cradling his ass as he thrust gently into my mouth, his thighs clenching around my head as he took his pleasure. I encouraged him to move faster, focusing on breathing, keeping my teeth off of his thick cock, and opening my throat to accept his appendage.

I swallowed around him, earning a shaky sob from above me, and then I hummed in appreciation as I felt pre-cum drip down my throat. I reached up, pressing my fingers to his lips. He opened automatically, his pants breathy as his eyes rolled back in their sockets. His fingers continued to clench my hair, making my eyes water with the sting. I gathered up as much spit as I could from his mouth, and then dropped my fingers down to his ass.

I pressed one finger against his hole and he was shuddering, moaning against me. He froze for a moment, but when my finger pressed inside of him, he began to thrust hesitantly again. I closed my eyes, reveling in the feel of him using my body to bring himself pleasure.

Before long, his pace had reached frantic. With each thrust forward, I swallowed and hummed, and when he jerked back he fucked himself back on my finger. I was up to the second knuckle when I added another finger. He hissed but didn't even pause in his thrusts. Looking up, watching his debauched face contort as he fucked himself back on my fingers and forward into my mouth, I had to fight back the urge to come completely untouched. When I pushed a third finger in, I swallowed him down, moaned against his sensitive cock, and thrust with all three fingers against his prostate. He came with a shriek, his cum shooting down my throat and his ass clenching so tightly on my fingers I stilled them, afraid I would hurt him. I swallowed each drop of his cum down, smiling and humming against him until he pulled back with a gentle, breathy laugh. I gingerly pulled my fingers from his ass, rubbing my hands up and down his back as he calmed against me.

"Do you still want this, little wolf? I can easily spend the rest of my life tasting your cum and be a perfectly sated man."

His grunt of amusement rumbled across my skin and then he was holding himself above me, his arms on either side of my head, and his smile was dazzling. He thrust his softening, wet and twitching dick against my belly, chuckling when I groaned.

"I'm sure, Lhiam," he answered with a wicked light in his eyes. "I want to feel you inside me. I want to feel you and only you."

I nodded, and began the enjoyable process of arousing him again.

23- Willing and Free

E^{DON}

When I came down his throat, I thought I would never be able to get hard again. I thought he had sucked me dry of cum.

I had been wrong.

Within only a few minutes of emptying inside of his talented mouth, Lhiam had me rock hard again, my throbbing cock jutting up against my belly, begging to be touched. With only his fingers, tongue and teeth against my nipples, and a few hot-as-hell kisses, I was begging for his cock. I barely even noticed him grabbing the oil, but when I felt his three fingers, coated in oil, slipping back inside of me, I hoped I could last long enough for him to get inside of me. That spot inside of me he had teased in the bath, and again while I fucked his face, was throbbing as he rubbed around it, spreading his fingers out to stretch me for his entry, but he never quite touched it straight on.

I felt him reach for the oil again, and then his mouth was back on mine, his tongue owning every inch of my mouth. When I was gasping his name, thrusting blindly against the air and then back against his fingers, he pulled out, staring into my eyes.

"Are you ready, little wolf?" he asked, and I nodded emphatically.

I had never known the sensations that washed through my body at his touch, and never had a man prepared me like this. I knew it would still hurt when he thrust inside me, but I was willing to bite my tongue through the pain, because I wanted that for him. I wanted to give him everything, so that pain was a small price for me to pay.

But when the tip of his cock pressed against my hole, I froze, all thought of Lhiam fleeing, replaced by a smothered mouth, heaving breaths, muffled screams, and the rot of dirty flesh slapping against mine. I fought against the restraints, wanting only away from the stench and the pain and the shame. But I couldn't get free. I couldn't—

"Edon," Lhiam's voice filtered through the haze my mind had become, his eyes coming into focus as I blinked down at him. "Come back to me, little wolf. Keep your eyes open and on me, alright? Don't look away. Know that it's me here with you. Me and no other."

I nodded, staring down at eyes filled with empathy, strength and adoration. And with that, my flagging cock was back at full mast and I shuddered as the head of his dick pressed through the first ring of muscle in my ass. Lhiam froze, his muscles visibly straining below me, as he watched my face so closely I felt a blush heat my cheeks.

"Keep going," I whispered, afraid to break this moment with words. Because words weren't enough to express everything I was feeling:

Empowered, as I hovered over him, watching his body strain with holding himself back. This powerful, strong man was losing control... because of me. Lust like I had never felt before. Affection for the beautiful, selfless man who was willing to put his pleasure on hold so he didn't hurt me. And a soul-deep need to be closer to him. To make him mine. To claim him, mark him, make certain that any that came upon him knew to whom he belonged.

One hand clenching my hip to hold me steady, the other gripping his cock to press into me, Lhiam thrust in a bit more before pulling back, then back in again. With each thrust in, he was buried a bit deeper, and before long my ass was flush with his thighs and I was whimpering, impaled completely on his cock.

There was a hot, tingling stretch, and an over fullness that was strangely pleasant, but no pain. I kept my eyes open, even though everything in me wanted to throw my head back, close my eyes, and moan. But I kept my eyes on Lhiam, afraid that if I looked away I would lose myself to my demons again.

"Alright?" Lhiam breathed, the hand that had been gripping his cock reaching up to brush hair from my face. I nodded, feeling the cock inside my body pressing up against that spot inside when Lhiam shifted. I cried out, my hands falling down to clutch Lhiam's chest. He watched me for a moment, studying me, and then smiled.

"Feels good?" he murmured, before pulling back an inch and thrusting back in.

Nothing could have prepared me for the shot of heat and overwhelming pleasure when his dick rubbed up against that spot with the move. I moaned again, and Lhiam brought his hand up, twining our fingers together before dragging me down so my chest was flush with his. Our joined hands resting by his head, Lhiam began a steady, slow thrusting up into my body while I shuddered and moaned above him.

His eyes never left mine, watching me fall apart. He dragged my mouth down and swallowed down my moans as pre-cum dripped from my cock onto his stomach. I whimpered with a particularly harsh thrust and he yanked his head back, but when he saw my face he smiled.

"So sexy, little wolf," he moaned, sweat dripping down his forehead and back into his hair. I sat back against him and he lifted his knees so I could lean back against his thighs. I held myself up, then he grabbed both of my hands, entwining our fingers again, and I used his hands as leverage to lift myself up and impale myself on his thick cock, over and over.

It wasn't long before I was riding the edge of my orgasm, my entire body tight with an agony of pleasure. There was no pain, only flashes of heat and an almost unbearable fullness. A completeness I knew instinctively I would only feel with my prince.

When Lhiam pulled one of his hands from mine, I almost growled at the loss of contact, but then his hand was gripping my cock and I could barely breathe as my orgasm continued to build.

"Oh gods, Lhiam," I growled, fighting to keep my eyes on him as my lunges forward pressed me against his palm, and my thrusts back impaled me on his dick and sent a rush of heat down my spine. "Please. So hot. Too much. I can't..." My voice broke and I couldn't continue as Lhiam began to meet my thrusts back with an upward drive of his hips. I could feel tears pouring down my face, but I couldn't stop them. Lhiam brushed them from my cheeks, his eyes soft as he panted beneath me, bringing my hand down to press against his chest, just above his heart.

The move was a substitute for the words he held back, and I immediately understood. He wasn't fucking me. And this wasn't just making love. It was more. So, so much more.

It was freedom. And it was taking back everything every single one of those men had stolen from me. It was an act of defiance, a war cry, a rebel outpouring of rage. I belonged only to myself; my body was mine.

And I was sharing it— willingly— with a beautiful man who understood what the act meant to me. What this moment meant for my soul, for my mind, and for my heart.

I was free. And they hadn't broken me.

Within a few more of Lhiam's shoves up against me, I was coming in his hand, my ass clenching down on his cock inside me. My entire body seized as I broke apart, my mind shattering as pleasure exploded inside my veins, drowning everything else out as I screamed.

My cries were soon followed by Lhiam's grunts as he jolted his hips a few more times in my tight sheath, and then the wet heat that filled my body from his release had aftershocks rocking me back. My back arched against my will, and my fingers clutched against Lhiam's so tightly I feared I was hurting him.

When the orgasm began to recede, and the aftershocks were less frequent, I whimpered as I slumped against Lhiam's chest, his cock slowly softening inside my body. I could feel his copious release dripping out of me around his cock, but I ignored it, content to lie and enjoy his body wrapped around mine as my own shivered in ecstasy against him.

24- Little Wolf

L HIAM

Edon falling apart above me was the most exquisite sight I had ever had the pleasure of viewing. I was in awe of his body, thrashing above me, seeking out his pleasure using my body. And giving me so much in return. He was allowing me to be a part of reclaiming his soul. And I reveled in it.

I could see him fall away from me the moment my cock touched his hole. But with soft touches and gentle words, I brought him back enough that we could continue. I watched him closely the whole time, every time a moan from his mouth sounded higher-pitched, every time he twitched sporadically, I made sure he hadn't been pulled back under.

But he stayed with me, his eyes never leaving mine. And when he shattered I followed him soon after. When I came back into my body, Edon's weight on my chest was like a calming balm. My cock had slipped from his hole, and I could feel my cum cooling against it, making me shiver. My plan when we had begun was to pull out before I could come, so I wouldn't dirty him, but that idea had been shot to hell the moment my cock was fully encased in his tight sheath. Because there wasn't a chance in hell I could've pulled from him to save my life. Only Edon's words could have pulled me from him, but he never asked.

It wasn't until I woke with Edon squirming atop me that I realized we had fallen to sleep with our release crusting on our bodies. I smiled drowsily down at Edon and groaned when his belly rubbed against my rock hard cock.

"Good morning," he murmured, bringing his lips hesitantly to mine and brushing them against me with a tenderness that had my heart squeezing in my chest.

"Good morning, little wolf," I answered, my voice pathetically high pitched in my own ears. I looked over at the window and saw that the sun was high in the sky, so at least we had only slept for a few hours, at most. "How do you feel?"

His blush spread across his face like a wildfire and I chuckled as he ducked his head down and nipped at my chest in embarrassment.

"Amazing," he whispered against my skin, and I shook my head to hold back another groan.

"Little wolf, unless you want to repeat our performance from earlier, can you scoot up a bit? Your gorgeous ass is rubbing against my dick and it's liable to get smacked if it keeps it up."

Edon laughed out loud, pulling away to stare down into my eyes. A mischievous glint lighted in those amber depths, and he slowly, sensuously rolled his hips, dragging my cock along his taint. I hissed, arching my back and trying my hardest not to thrust up against him. I gripped his shoulders, wrapping my legs around his knees and dragging him down so he lay flat on his back as I hovered above him. I held myself up with my arms around his neck, caging him in with my body. The panic in his eyes was clear, but brief. Replaced by an affectionate smile and a wet kiss against the closest part of me he could reach— my forearm.

"And if I say I want a repeat?"

He had barely finished before I was slicked with oil and slowly pressing myself inside of him.

The second time was slower, gentler, less manic. Less about his past, his pain, his defiance, than it was about discovering each other. We tasted each other, running hands and tongues and lips over each other's body. I didn't turn Edon onto his belly, because I knew he may never be comfortable with that position, but every other bit of his skin I could reach I lathered with affection. I kept up a constant rolling of my hips, and when he came with a soft cry beneath me, I stilled inside of him so as not to overstimulate his prostate. We kissed, our tongues dancing, teeth nipping, lips pressing against each other, until he was writhing beneath me again.

When he came again, it was with an almost pained cry, and I followed him down with a groan that was ripped directly from my belly.

After I managed to clean the release and oil from both of our bodies with a wet towel, we spent the rest of the day into the evening in each other's arms. Not having sex again, but making love. Kissing, touching, simply lying in the warmth of each other's arms.

When Robert brought our dinner, knocking on the door with obvious hesitation, both Edon and I apologized to the guard. He seemed concerned with Edon, especially since the young man now looked completely debauched. I would have been offended that he thought I would ever force someone into my bed, if I hadn't been so impressed with his gumption and compassion.

The moment he moved into the room, I could see his dark eyes light on the rumpled sheets, the very naked wolf boy, who, as had always been the case, barely even noticed he was naked as he jumped from the bed, and then to me. He glared at me before turning to Edon, who was eagerly helping the man set the tray on the table near the bed.

"Are you alright, kid?" he asked, drawing a blush from Edon, who nodded fervently. I wondered for a moment what the guard would do if Edon answered in the negative and I had my answer when Robert turned to glare at me again.

He may have left earlier at my command, but if Edon requested his help, or even voiced a concern, he wouldn't turn his back on him.

And I was proud of the man for that. I would never hurt Edon, so I had nothing to worry about, but it was good to know I had a man near me that was so willing to do the right thing, no matter what it meant.

"I'm really alright," Edon murmured, his eyes flickering from Robert to me and then back again. "I'm sorry about before. I get... scared, sometimes. But it wasn't Lhia... it wasn't His Highness' fault at all."

Robert studied Edon for another moment before turning back to me, his eyes a bit softer, and bowed, and then he twirled back on Edon.

"If you ever need anything, please know you have a friend in me, kid," he said simply. And then he ruffled the hair back out of Edon's face before turning his back on him and exiting as quickly as he had come in.

"I'm sorry I embarrassed you, Your Highness," Edon muttered, and I rolled my eyes before joining him at the table. Neither of us wore clothes, but since I knew we would just be taking them off after we'd eaten, I didn't mind my nakedness.

"You did no such thing. Robert was only looking out for you. I'm grateful, actually. It's good to know he's that kind of man."

"'That kind of man?'" Edon repeated as he began to chew thoughtfully on a soft buttered roll.

"The kind of man that will help someone in need, in spite of who is the aggressor."

Edon thought for a moment, before a look of horror crossed his eyes.

"You mean you think he would betray you if he thought you were hurting me?"

"Exactly."

"But... that's not a good thing, Lhiam."

"It is, though," I stressed, smiling when he looked at me doubtfully. "The fact that he would go against even the ruler of his realm, to help someone in need? Even kings and princes can do evil things, Edon. And just because they were born into royalty doesn't mean they should be allowed to do whatever they want, regardless of whom they hurt. I'm grateful I have such a man looking out for my people."

Edon shrugged and shook his head. "If you say so."

I chuckled, lifting his hand to my lips to kiss his palm, and then dug into our meal.

We spent the entire rest of the night and well into the morning lost in each other's bodies. I spent the better part of an hour around midnight rimming Edon's ass, my tongue fucking into his soft hole, drawing gasps and groans from him as he gripped the bedsheets around his head, his legs spread eagle beneath me. Using only my tongue and a few gentle drags across his prostate with the tips of my fingers, I continuously dragged him to the edge of orgasm before easing off. When he was a babbling mess above me, his toes digging into the bed as his back arched perfectly beneath my hands, begging me to let him come with incoherent ramblings, I sucked at his hole while digging my nose into his taint and gently cupping his balls, and he was shooting a load of cum up across his belly with his cock untouched.

When Edon managed to drag himself back from the orgasm, I worked his body up again before opening him up on my cock with a copious amount of oil. He came twice more on my cock, once again with his cock completely untouched, with only my hard member continuously rubbing against his prostate and the sensitive nerves of his ass to bring him to the peak. I followed him down through his second orgasm around my cock, third in an hour, and felt my release flood his insides with a spark of pride.

Mine.

I slept for only a few hours before I had to get up to attend a meeting. It had been called by Stefan, and I knew it was about the princess he had invited, who was arriving later that day. Just another in a long line of potential brides for me.

Unlike all the others, however, I was truly furious about this one. I knew Stefan had heard the rumors of my affection for Edon— Tate's "cousin"— and that was why his efforts had redoubled in regards to a wife for me. I intended to make it clear to Stefan that I would treat this current princess with the respect due her station, but she would be the last. Because one way or another, I would never marry a woman, much less one picked out for me for political reasons.

Because I had found the person I was going to marry, and it had nothing to do with politics or my country. Edon was in my heart, and my soul, and I belonged to him wholly. I could only pray that he would agree to belong to me in every way as well. It was early, I knew, but there was something about Edon that made me forget about what many saw as normal and just want to tie him to me in any way I could.

I also knew he still hesitated because of our gender and our stations, so I hoped that asking him to marry me would soothe those doubts. I would claim him before all, and I prayed that would be enough to get him to stay.

I had already spoken to Lacy about Edon and my plans to ask him to be my husband, and she had agreed that I should give him my mother's— her grandmother's— wedding ring. It should rightfully belong to my wife or to Lacy, but I had received Lacy's delighted approval to give the small, carved silver ring to Edon.

I kissed Edon's warm, sleepy cheek as I pulled myself from his body that had so affectionately wrapped around mine. He whimpered in his sleep, his body trying to follow mine instinctively, and it was one of the hardest things I had ever done to move away from him and dress. I bathed and dressed as quietly as I could, and Edon only woke when I was ready to go and had to kiss his lips one more time before I left the room.

As I pressed my lips to his, his eyes fluttered open and he sighed as he returned the kiss, still half asleep.

"Stay in bed, my love," I murmured against his lips. "I'll be back in a few hours."

He mumbled inarticulately, and I chuckled at the childish, sleepy way he glared up at me.

"Come back... bed," he grumbled, pulling my neck down to plaster his mouth against mine wetly. I chuckled again as I melted into the kiss, then pulled myself away and tucked the blankets around him.

"Rest. I have a meeting. I'll be back as soon as I can."

25- Disgusting Rumors

E^{DON}

I drifted in and out of sleep after Lhiam left but woke fully when
the sun was high in the sky. It took me a few minutes to realize that I had
actually slept more than a few hours the night before, and I knew it was all
thanks to Lhiam. It wasn't just that he had exhausted my body— because
gods, what that man could do with his tongue and his hands and his cock
had me squirming at even the thought— but I was safe with him. I felt
safer in his arms than I had ever felt.

I slunk from the bed, dressing as quickly as I could, and made my way out
to the south garden. If it was noon, which I suspected it was due to the
sun's alignment in the sky, Lacy would be having lunch in the garden. And
I was certain she would share.

My growling stomach demanded it.

"Nice to see you up and moving around, kid," Robert said, clapping me on
the back when I entered the garden's gate. He stood watch over Lacy, who
knelt on a small blanket, daintily chewing on a vegetable sandwich.

"Edon!" she called when she caught sight of me. She jumped up, running at me and throwing her arms around my waist. I stiffened, even now, after dozens of these hugs from the girl, thrown off by the affection I felt in her arms. She squeezed tightly and then pulled back, looking up at me with sparkling eyes. "I'm so glad you're alright! Lhiam wouldn't let me come see you. He wouldn't let anyone in the room; stupid, overprotective men."

I flinched at the words, at another reminder that Lhiam was ashamed of me, was keeping me, and our relationship, a secret. Like I was something shameful. Something dirty he couldn't let anyone know he was fucking. I hoped the child hadn't noticed the move. But I knew she had, because she was suddenly frowning and dragging me to her blanket.

"Sit, Edon. I don't have any meat, because I didn't know you would be joining me. But a vegetable sandwich won't hurt you."

I chuckled and gratefully accepted the sandwich and the apple she lobbed over to me.

"I'm so glad you and my cousin finally got past your individual stupidities," Lacy said suddenly, just as I took the first bite of my sandwich. I stared at her, trying to keep my mouth from hanging open, and could feel a deep blush run across my face. "I'm surprised to see you up and about. And with only the smallest hint of a limp."

"Lacy!" I finally managed to choke out, and the girl dissolved into giggles, clutching her stomach as she shook her head. Robert's soft laughter behind me made me want to dig myself into a hole.

"You should see your face, Edon!" she gasped, wiping at her eyes, as if to brush away tears of mirth. "What, you think I don't know what you two have been up to for near two days? I happen to know, from sources I will not name, mind you, that you woke from your injuries almost two days ago. I'm not a child, Edon."

I glared over at Robert, who was adamantly refusing to meet my eyes, but also hadn't stopped laughing, and then back to Lacy.

"I'm glad," she whispered, and I had to strain my ears to hear her words. "My cousin deserves happiness, and you make him so happy, Edon. I'm glad we found you. I'm glad you're here. I'm glad you seem to feel the same way—"

"— Lacy," I cut in, laying the bitten sandwich on the cloth she had set out for me. I shook my head, trying to clear my thoughts. How could I explain to this child something that tore my heart open each time I thought of it? How could I explain to her that her cousin and I could never take our relationship further than the bedchamber? It wasn't something I was comfortable explaining to a girl her age. "Lacy, it's not like that. Your cousin and I... "

I shook my head, unable to find the words, but Lacy was staring at me as if I had spat in her face.

"You do not love Lhiam?" she asked gently, her eyes widening in horror as some kind of realization hit her at her own words. "Edon! You didn't... You didn't sleep with Lhiam because you felt... indebted to him, did you? Oh no, he's going to be—"

"No!" I yelled, shaking my head and clasping my hands in my lap to keep them from shaking. "No, Lacy, it's not that. You must understand, I'm.... Lhiam is..."

"He loves you," she said sternly, her confusion and anger apparent. "If you feel the same, and I think you do, then I don't see what—"

"Ah, Your Highness, there you are!"

Stefan's portly body followed his voice as he rounded the gate and nodded congenially at Robert. He completely ignored me, which I was used to, as he held his hand out to Lacy.

"Your cousin needs you in the council chambers," he said, offering no other explanation. I noticed a tall woman standing beside Robert, her attention fixed on Lacy as well. She was stunning, with long, rolling blonde hair, porcelain features, and red-as-sin lips. She smelled of rose water and gold, but it wasn't a pleasant smell.

I could almost see the eye roll Lacy held back as she took Stefan's hand and looked down at me.

"I'll be back soon. Do you mind...?" She gestured at her little picnic and I nodded wordlessly, agreeing to clean it.

"Don't clean it up just yet," Stefan said, still not even looking at me. "The Lady Tracy and I will be waiting out here for a while, until the meeting is over. I'm sure the lady is hungry after her travels...?"

The woman nodded, smiling gently and moving to the bench near the blanket where I still sat. Uncomfortable, I stood and began to follow Lacy, but a hand on my arm held me back. I fought back a growl at the unfamiliar touch.

"Stay with the Lady Tracy, guard," Stefan all but growled at me, his eyes flashing with something I could only call malice.

"Edon is my guard—" Lacy began, but Stefan ignored her words.

"Quickly, child. It took me a while to find you, so your cousin has been kept waiting. Robert, follow the princess, if you please."

Lacy met my eyes, and then huffed in frustration before disappearing. Robert only hesitated a moment, his eyes bouncing from the lady, to

Stefan, to me, and then back again, before he turned with a soft sigh. I moved as quickly as I could to take Robert's place beside the gate and wait for Lacy's return.

"I'm so glad you got here so quickly, my lady," Stefan simpered. I tried to tune out their words, but something about the way they were both positioned facing me, almost as if they intended to include me in their conversation, made it difficult not to hear, and process, every word they said.

"I'm glad for the opportunity, my Lord Stephan," she answered, her voice like silk dipped in honey. "I'm glad the prince is pleased with me."

"Very much so," the man answered with a smile as my stomach began to drop, as if my body understood before my brain could catch up. "He has put off marriage too long. The country needs an heir, and his highness has intimated his excitement for marriage. He has even pulled his parents' wedding rings out of storage, in preparation for your arrival. I hope you don't mind that it will be a quiet affair. His Highness does love his frugality, and he is a humble man. He will want something small and intimate, but I'm sure we can talk him into a few things, if we are very persuasive."

The woman laughed, her eyes flicking to me so quickly I thought I may have imagined it before she was blushing sweetly.

"I can be very persuasive, my lord," she giggled, and then her eyes were definitely meeting mine and I felt bile rise to my throat. "I believe my persuasiveness will be a fine trait that will aid His Highness in the throne room, as well as the bedroom."

"I'm sure, I'm sure," Stefan said, laughing and patting her hand. "As long as you give him heirs, whatever else you two do with your spare time is up to you."

The pair laughed again, and my gut twisted. I had to get out. I couldn't be here. I wasn't meant to hear this. I couldn't hear anymore. I turned, grabbing at my chest, trying to hold back the agony that was piercing through me, but the woman's voice stopped me in my tracks.

"And what of these distasteful rumors, my lord?" she whispered, her voice so quiet I had to strain my ears to hear. "That he is... bedding a man?" She shuddered dramatically, and then, "Disgusting."

"I will not lie to you, child. They are true enough. But if I know the prince, and I do, he will set aside the boy once you are engaged officially. He is besotted with the boy, but it is just a fascination with a new toy. He will remember his duty and the boy will be gone. You have my word. The boy will be sent away before the ink dries on the wedding contract."

The woman paused for a moment, as if deliberating, and then she sighed softly, almost heart brokenly. "I suppose, if he must have his dirty indiscretions, a man is the way to go. At least that way there isn't any chance for bastards. As long as I never have to set my eyes on the man, I can be... flexible with my husband. And as long as he cares for me properly, as his wife, he can keep whatever whores he wants outside of our marriage bed."

The twisting in my gut grew almost violent as I doubled over.

"Boy," the woman's voice called, and I glanced back at her. She was blurry, and I realized it was because there were tears pouring from my eyes. I hadn't even noticed. "Whatever is the matter, boy?"

But the malice in her words told me she knew. She knew who I was. She knew I was the filthy whore her husband would sully their marriage with. And she was proving to me just where I belonged. Bent over and fucked in dark corners, in secret, outside of a proper marriage bed.

NO.

My entire body was wracked with shaking as I backed away and ran. I wanted to shift, but the emotions that were running through my body were too much for my wolf. They would stop his heart. So I ran on bare feet until I found a small enclave behind a thick tapestry. I shoved myself into the hole, wrapping my body around itself as tightly as I could, and let the tears take over.

I could barely breathe past the images of the beautiful woman, a child on her hip, her belly full with another, as Lhiam reached down to kiss her. His hand on her belly, his eyes lit with laughter and joy. And then the images changed to Lhiam in a dark, dirty room, my body bent over a desk, his hips pounding into me hurriedly as he secretly fucked his whore.

No. I couldn't do it. I had entertained thoughts of being alright with being his dirty secret and had even known that someday he would take a wife. But now that the time had come, my heart was tearing open at even the thoughts of what my future held if I stayed.

I couldn't do it. I couldn't be his secret. I couldn't watch on from the shadows as he lived and loved, and never be able to step into the light.

I had to leave. And I had to do it so he didn't know until it was too late. Because I feared that with only a few words, Lhiam could tear me open and I would stay just to be near his voice, near to his warmth and his soul. That with only a few words, Lhiam could convince me to stay with him, at the cost of my heart and soul.

And I would slowly die, over years and years.

So I would give myself one more night. I would love Lhiam, give myself to him one more time. I would pretend, for one night, that he loved me, that I wasn't his dirty secret, that he belonged to me, and I to him, and that the world wasn't a cruel, dark place.

And then I would tear my own heart open and leave, because that's what I should have done weeks ago.

Because I had felt, the moment I met him, that he would break me the way my Masters had tried and failed to.

And that premonition was coming true. In ways more painful than I ever could have imagined.

The sun had set before I managed to drag myself back to Lhiam's rooms. Robert and Cain stood guard outside the door, and both nodded as I pushed my way inside. Lacy and Lhiam laughed and chatted, sitting at the table just in front of the fire. They both looked up when I entered, and I felt a small piece of my heart shear off when Lhiam smiled so brightly at me. As if I was the only thing he could see. As if I was special.

As if I was worth the shame that sullying his marriage by fucking me would bring.

I tried to return their smiles, but I couldn't get my lips to cooperate. I only prayed my face wasn't red and puffy from my afternoon of sobbing. And that neither would see the determination and the decision in my eyes.

Lacy frowned as she studied me, but Lhiam only called out to me to join them.

"I ate already," I lied, flinching when my voice came out rough and gravelly.

"I was going to sleep soon, anyways," Lacy whispered, her confused, hesitant eyes on me as she rose and kissed her cousin's cheek. "You two have a good night."

She moved to me, sadness in her scent as she looked deeply into my eyes.

"Please don't break his heart, Edon," she whispered, so quietly I knew Lhiam couldn't hear her. "If you don't... If you don't feel the same way, let him know gently. Please, Edon."

I nodded, refusing to meet her eyes, and she disappeared through the door with a sigh.

"Is everything alright?" Lhiam murmured, his eyes on the door behind me, and then turning back to me with confusion. But there was still joy in his eyes when he looked on me. He had sensed something, but he wasn't close to guessing.

Good.

I had to distract him before he forced me to lay bare my heart to him with only a few glances and words. Because his power over me was that absolute.

I moved towards him steadily, ignoring the tearing sensations in my chest and the shaking of my hands.

"Need you, Lhiam," I murmured, wrapping my arms around his neck and pulling him down to me for a wet, possessive kiss. He let me control it, jamming my tongue into his mouth and sucking his into my own.

When I finally pulled away, he took a deep breath and opened his eyes. His eyes, when they met mine, were filled with lust, need, and affection.

I ignored the way my soul cried out in agony.

This can't be the last time!

It has to be, my mind whimpered back.

"Please, Lhiam," I whispered against his lips. "I need you... I need to be inside of you. Please give everything to me. I'll be so good for you, Lhiam."

He didn't even hesitate before he answered. "Of course, little wolf. Anything you want, I am yours."

I gasped as his words shredded my heart and my knees almost gave out, but I refused to back down. I would have this. Him. For tonight. And the memories would have to last me the rest of my life. He was mine— if for only one night. If only for these next few moments, for as long as I could allow myself to linger.

He was mine as I said goodbye.

26- Too Much

There was something wrong, but I could only guess until Edon found the courage to talk to me about it. And if letting him have this piece of myself I had never given to another was the way to get him to open to me, then I wouldn't even hesitate. It's not as if I had never planned to allow Edon to penetrate me, it simply hadn't come up yet.

And the possessive, hungry way he was kissing me, holding me while his mouth ravaged my own, was sending bursts of lust and hope through my body. Had he finally pushed past his insecurities, and was claiming me? Or was he simply hornier than he had been before?

I couldn't tell. Besides the lusty and grasping way he was devouring me, he was expressionless. Closed off. As if afraid I might be able to read his mind.

We made our way to the bed, lips and teeth and tongues and fingers grasping, biting, tasting. When he had managed to rip my clothes from my body, he shoved me onto the bed and followed me down, tearing his shirt over his head as he growled down at me.

"Edon," I gasped when he yanked me around, his hands stronger than I had known they could be as he bodily moved me with little effort. "Sweetheart, slow down. I'm right here. I'm not going anywhere. I'm here with you, my love."

The man whimpered, gently nipping at my ass cheek as he lowered himself down. I set the oil within his reach and then tried to relax. But that was shot to hell when his sharp fingernails— claws?— dug into my skin and pulled my cheeks apart, and his tongue was making its slow, hot way up my crease. I jerked and cried out, making Edon freeze. I looked back at him, saw the uncertainty in his gaze, as if afraid he had hurt me. I reassured him with a smile.

"Feels so good, little wolf," I whispered. He growled hungrily and then his tongue was everywhere, hot and insistent and so fucking good. I moaned, gasped, and tried to squirm, but his strong hands held me to the bed as he fucked my ass with his tongue.

It was only when I was rutting against the bed, begging incoherently, that he pulled his tongue from my body, only to be joined by a finger that slid in and out of my relaxed hole. He continued licking around his finger, dipping his tongue in beside it as he thrust in and out with the digit.

I cried out, shaking my head and biting at the pillow beneath me as his finger scraped my prostate. He added another within seconds and I had never felt so full, or so complete.

"Edon! Stop, I'm going to come! I want... I want you inside me when I come. Please, Edon!"

Edon pulled away, and I could hear him working the cork out of the bottle of oil, and then the liquid was dripping inside of me and the blunt head of his cock was pressed to my hole.

"Mine," he growled, pressing almost half of his cock inside of me with one thrust. I cried out in pain, reaching back to hold his hips still.

"Edon! Slowly! Go slowly, please, my love."

The man above me shuddered, his breaths raspy, growling with each exhale. I looked back, meeting his darkened eyes. There was something seriously wrong, but I couldn't deny him. Was he trying to get me to prove myself to him? Was he testing me?

I prayed I passed the test as I let my hand fall to the bed and the man began to steadily push himself inside of me. Slower and gentler than before. The pain was soon replaced by an overwhelming burn, and then a sensation I wanted to seek out. To bury myself in.

And then his hips were flush against my ass and Edon was whimpering and shaking so hard I felt it like vibrations in my sensitive ass.

"Mine," he growled again, this time sounding more human, more in control than he had before, and I smiled back at him over my shoulder.

"Yours," I agreed. "Only yours."

Edon studied me for a few minutes, his eyes covering my face, then the rest of my body, as if marking me in his mind, before he lowered himself down and brought his mouth over mine.

"Want my cum inside you," he hissed as his hips began a steady thrusting inside of me. The pain was almost completely gone, the intense burn and pleasure rushing through my blood. "Want to mark you. Mine."

"Yes," I breathed, knowing I wouldn't last much longer. He had brought me to the edge before pushing himself inside of me, and now I was back there again. I could feel my orgasm building, and he hadn't even touched my cock. "Yours. I'm yours. I want your cum inside me, little wolf. I need it."

Edon growled sharply as his hips sped up, his skin slapping against mine. He grabbed my hands, shoving them to the bed above my head and twisting our fingers together when I tried to reach underneath me to my cock. I whined, rutting back against him. He shifted his hips, and I screamed as he was now pressing directly against my prostate with each thrust into my body.

And just as I thought I was going to shatter, something tugged at my hole and I froze.

"Edon...?" I whispered as his thrusts became erratic, his panting against my ear sending lightning bolts down my spine. "Edon, what is... oh holy gods!"

My body exploded, my cum spurting into the blankets and sheets pressed up against me, just as Edon's body froze, his groin flush with my ass. Because he could no longer pull out at all. Something thick and heavy at the base of his cock had expanded, tying us together. I felt his hot release inside of me as he whimpered into my ear, his body falling limp against my back. I could feel he was biting down on the curve between my neck and my shoulder, but I could barely register the pain for the pleasure that lit every nerve ending on fire.

"Edon...?" I mumbled when I came back to myself, my body jerking with aftershocks as his hot liquid continued to spill inside of me. But with the word, he shifted, and the thickness in my body was pressed tightly against my prostate and I was miraculously coming again, my balls shooting out everything they could as I screamed into the pillow below me.

"Edon!" I screamed, jerking below him. I felt his hands stroking my back, my hair, soothing me. "Edon, it's... oh gods, too much!"

The orgasm was endless, sweeping through me and leaving me afraid I would never be able to catch my breath. But then I did, and Edon was there, his gentle kisses against my neck, my cheeks, my back soothing as I came down and back into his arms.

"Oh please, gods, don't move," I whimpered, but then my body jerked involuntarily as I felt another spurt of his cum inside my body and I blacked out as a third orgasm tore my body apart.

27- I'm Yours

E^{DON}

When Lhiam came to after only a few minutes, I was still inside of him. I was terrified I would make him come again, but my knot had deflated enough that I knew I wasn't pressing as violently against his prostate as I had been.

"I'm sorry, Lhiam," I whispered, gently licking his eyes free of the tears that had begun to flow again as he woke. "I didn't... I didn't know."

Lhiam looked back at me, his eyes wide with something I couldn't name. He twisted his body so he could eye the place where we were still connected, and then he chuckled, his voice dry and rough with his screams.

"Well," he said gently, pulling my arm so that it was wrapped around him, and then placing a gentle kiss to my fingers. "That's an interesting bit of anatomical information to find out mid-fuck."

I wanted to laugh, but I was still afraid I had hurt him.

"I'm sorry," I repeated, nuzzling the bite mark on his neck. He hadn't bled, but it was dark and bruised.

"I orgasmed three times in a row, because you knotted my ass like a wolf does to a bitch in heat. Please don't ever apologize for amazing, if kinky, sex, little wolf." He was chuckling gently, but I could smell the sleep beginning to take over him.

"In fact, I will have to insist that that happens again. Does this mean your body wants to mate me, wolf?" he asked sleepily. "Your wolf body wants to fill me with your pups?"

I groaned and bit down on his neck, fighting everything in me that was pushing my knot to inflate again, and he simply chuckled.

"I like that your body knows I'm yours," he whispered, and then his breaths were even with sleep and my heart was breaking open.

Because he had been mine. For those few moments, for the last two days, his body and affections had belonged wholly to me. And now I had to rejoin reality and walk away from the man who had finally succeeded in breaking me open so that I may never heal.

I wrapped my smaller body around Lhiam's as tightly as I could without waking him, cursing the damn knot for not allowing me to leave yet. I needed to get out. Now. And I couldn't leave until it went down. I couldn't hurt Lhiam, and I couldn't wake him.

I sobbed silently, my tears falling against Lhiam's skin, as I waited the almost 30 minutes for my knot to go down. After a few minutes, my sobs died down, and I had to fight to stay awake and not sleep against Lhiam's warm back. I used the time to revel in the feel of Lhiam's skin against my own, his warm breaths, his heartbeat loud against my ear.

But each second was tearing me apart.

When my knot was small enough for me to pull out without hurting Lhiam, I slid myself out of him as gently and slowly as I could, knowing I couldn't wake him. He whimpered in his sleep when my cock slipped from his hole, followed by a line of cum. I fought the urge to press it back inside, to keep that bit of myself inside of him, and the other, more dangerous one, to clean him off and wrap my body around his and stay in his arms. To wake by his side, wrapped around his body, in a few hours and let him do whatever he wanted with me, body and soul, no matter what pain it caused me.

But my self-preservation instincts kicked in. So I slid to the ground, covered him with the blankets, dressed as quickly and silently as I could, and made my way out of the room. I left behind all of the sets of clothes and boots Lhiam had made for me, keeping my feet bare and wearing only a pair of undergarments, a thin shirt and tunic, and a pair of breeches. None of the things Lhiam had bought me were mine. Not really. And each would remind me of the other half of my heart that I was leaving behind.

Robert was used to my nightly excursions, since that was how we had met, so he said nothing as I slipped past him just outside of Lhiam's door.

I ran into not another soul until I reached the southern gates that let out into the forest behind the keep. And there, I was stopped by a voice I had dreaded hearing almost as much as Lhiam's.

"Did you even say goodbye to him?" Lacy whispered, stepping out of the shadows. I should have sensed her, smelled her, but my mind was far too distracted. I could smell the tears dripping down her face as her voice broke on her next words. "Were you going to say goodbye to me?"

I had no words, so I stayed silent. But inside, I was dying. Gods, I had never felt pain like this.

"You're a coward, Edon," she hissed, slapping at the tears on her cheeks as she glared up at me. "I thought you were braver than this. I thought you were... stronger than this."

"I am a coward," I answered, fighting back my own tears and turning my back on her. "Forget me, Your Highness. I'm not worth remembering. For either of you."

She gasped, and I turned back around, because it wasn't a sound that fit our situation. It was more a sound of pain than—

But that was my last thought as something slammed against the side of my face and I knew only darkness.

When I woke it was to blinding pain in my head, blood dripping steadily down my cheek, and agony in my shoulders. I remembered flashes of travel, horses, a girl screaming my name, and I jerked as everything came back.

"Lacy!" I yelled, my vision coming to me slowly. I was in a large tent, with a pole holding the middle up. I was tied to the pole, my arms above my head, and I was naked but for the small undergarments covering my groin.

A whimpering sigh to my side drew my eyes to the girl who was tied on a pile of pillows just below my feet.

Her mouth was gagged with a dirty cloth, and her eyes were red and soaked with tears.

Another scent in the tent drew my eyes to a large man who sat and watched me, his eyes seeming to glow in the lamplight.

"Good morning," the man said with amusement, but then he completely ignored me as he moved over and lifted Lacy easily with one hand on her upper arm. I growled, but I couldn't find words. My head was pounding, and I couldn't even scream as the girl was dragged over and pressed down onto a pile of blankets and pillows.

A bed.

No.

"No," I groaned, drawing the man's eyes and attention. "No, don't... don't hurt her. Please."

The man chuckled, shoving the girl back. She stared up at me, terror in her eyes so bright I feared losing her. Because I knew, from firsthand experience, that the terror was fleeting. And it was usually replaced by the pain, then the disgust and degradation and hopelessness, and finally the numbness, the empty apathy, and that was what I feared for my beautiful, precocious charge.

"Me," I hissed, the words still difficult to find, my mind keeping them just out of reach. "I'm good, Master. I'll be good for you. Won't... won't cry. Won't fight. I'm trained. The girl will fight. She doesn't know... how to make you feel so good, Master. Not like I do."

The man froze, his eyes looking me up and down, and then a disgusting, but familiar, gleam lit his eyes and he was moving towards me.

"You're offering me your ass for her pussy, boy?"

"Yes Master," I answered, lowering my voice as seductively as I could. I had never seduced someone before. Not even Lhiam. With him, he wanted me already. There had been no words needed, and no need to flatter or convince.

But I needed this man to want me over the small, beautiful girl he would rape if I didn't succeed. I had to make him need me, more than he wanted the virginity of a child.

"You a trained whore, boy?"

"Yes, Master," I answered, the words acid on my tongue. I tried to ignore Lacy's horrified eyes on me, her hands covering her mouth. It wouldn't matter that she knew now, because the likelihood of us getting out alive was so low, my own next to nil. "Trained since I was a child. Younger than the girl. I'll make it so good for you, Master."

The man smiled, the motion filled with more evil than I had seen in weeks.

Since the last time I had seen my Master.

"You disappoint me, I'll beat you and then go for the girl anyways, you understand me?"

I nodded, hoping I looked eager, and the man reached behind his back, pulled out a knife, and cut the ropes binding me to the pole. I briefly considered shifting and killing him, but now that my mind was clearing somewhat, I could smell the two dozen men outside the tent, and I knew that would only bring my and Lacy's death. I could probably kill this man, but not the dozens of men who would come to avenge his death.

Lacy was sobbing, curled into a ball on the bed as the man grabbed my arm and dragged me towards her.

"Get back in the corner, girl!" the man growled out. I met Lacy's eyes, putting a warning in mine. She needed to obey, or he may hurt her anyways. She slipped from the bed, and her soft hand brushing against mine nearly broke me.

I squeezed her hand back, and then let the man push me onto the bed. I reached for his pants as he began nipping and licking at my neck.

28- Sing Me That Song

✱ **Ok, so I know I said no more trigger warnings... But like, major trigger warning***

LHIAM

Waking without a warm bundle of wolf boy in my arms was disappointing, but I knew I should probably get used to it. Edon had a hard time sleeping, and that may never change. Not with everything he had been through in his life.

I reached over, sliding the drawer to the side of the bed open to pull out the soft velvet bag that held my future. I pulled the ornate silver ring from the bag and studied it.

My plan was to ask Edon tonight. I had told the council the day before, in no uncertain terms, that Lacy was my heir, and any children she eventually begat had full rights to the throne after her. I had also been firm when I told them that no further marriage talks would even be tolerated or humored.

As I studied the ring in my palm, I pictured Edon's reaction when I gave it to him, but I was at a loss. After last night, and the way he had... claimed me, I wasn't so sure he wouldn't be ecstatic by the public claiming. I could feel myself blush as I shifted and my hole was still wet with his copious release, and there was a soft twinge of pain from the passionate way he had taken me.

But other things held me back. His past, his fear of intimacy, his low self-esteem. I wasn't sure if he would even agree, much less be happy about being my husband.

But I had to ask. Because I wanted to belong to him, wanted him to be mine, for the rest of our lives. And I couldn't hold back from that anymore.

A heavy pounding on my door made me jerk and drop the ring. I picked it up off my chest, hiding it back in the pouch and the drawer and sitting up before I yelled "enter!"

I was ashamed at the disappointment I felt when it was Robert and Tate standing in the doorway rather than Edon, but the looks on their faces had me throwing the blankets from my naked body and standing quickly.

"Your Highness, we can't find Lacy," Tate said. My heart dropped as I began to pull on the clothes that Edon had ripped from me and thrown around the room the night before.

"Get Edon. He may be able to find—"

"—Your Highness, Edon left your room late last night and I was the last to see him," Robert cut in, his eyes wide as he gripped his sword.

The pain in my chest became a spear of agony and I clutched the bedpost to hold myself up.

"No," I hissed, my mind reeling. "Are they together, somewhere in town, or—"

"Edon always informs us if they're leaving for town or anywhere beyond the keep," Robert stated. "Lacy's maids have been searching since midnight."

"And I'm just now finding out!"

"Your cousin isn't exactly known for letting people know where she's going!" Tate defended with frustration. "If we told you every time she disappeared—"

"I understand," I growled, belting my sword to my waist. "You're right."

"I was informed once the maids realized Edon was gone too," Tate said gently.

"Fuck," I groaned, and shoving my heart and the emotions that threatened to overwhelm me back, I began issuing orders.

They didn't even turn out to be difficult to find. Within a few hours, reports came back of a large group of mercenaries that had passed through just outside of town. Being at least 30 strong, they left behind quite a trail once we found it, and they weren't moving fast.

Which I prayed and feared meant that they didn't know whom they had taken. It was highly likely that Lacy had been wearing her nightgown, or even a simple homespun dress as she was want to, so they likely thought they had taken a castle maid who wouldn't be missed. I hoped for this, because it meant she would still be alive.

But I feared it for the state she would almost definitely be in.

With each mile we pounded past, I thanked the gods that we didn't find Edon's body. I didn't know why they would be keeping him alive, but I thanked the gods they were. And prayed he wasn't back in a situation that would bring back to the forefront the nightmares in his mind.

I rode with a small contingent of only 20 men, but they were my best veterans, many of whom had fought by my side in battle. There were 30 more bringing up our rear, but we had left before them to get to Lacy and Edon quicker.

We came upon their camp almost 4 hours since I woke without Edon in my arms. We stayed in the shadows and the trees, waiting for the men coming behind us, but I quickly homed in on the large captain's tent near the fire. I could soon hear voices from inside, and my breath left me in a rush. But my joy at hearing a seemingly unharmed Lacy and Edon was soon replaced by horror and bile as I began to make out the words from the tent.

Edon's voice was quiet, and there was pain and a bit of hesitation and confusion, as if he had just woken, but his words were clear and even a little husky, seductive.

"I'm good, Master," he simpered, and my horror that he was offering himself to a man was quickly replaced with dawning dread as he continued. "I'll be good for you. Won't... won't cry. Won't fight. I'm trained. The girl will fight. She doesn't know... how to make you feel so good, Master. Not like I do."

I wanted more than anything to tear into the tent and rip the man apart, but I couldn't. Not only would it only endanger Lacy and Edon's life, but the lives of my men as well. Until our reinforcements arrived, we were sorely outnumbered. I felt Tate's hand on my arm, and I nodded.

I would hold back. He could trust me.

"You're offering me your ass for her pussy, boy?" the man's voice grunted, clearly intrigued. I imagined Edon's soft eyes, his stunning, red lips, his lithe body, and I knew that the man was coveting what was mine.

"Yes, Master," Edon answered, and my heart broke for him. Because of me. Because of Lacy, he was right back to what he had escaped from.

"You a trained whore, boy?"

"Yes, Master," Edon said again, and I could almost feel Robert, Tate and a few other men fight back their anger. Tate's hand on my arm grew almost painful. My entire body was shaking, but I was helpless. I could do nothing for my heart, my soul, the man who was giving himself up for the girl who was like my daughter. "Trained since I was a child. Younger than the girl. I'll make it so good for you, Master."

I finally couldn't hold back, and I spewed vomit into the bush to my right. I kept myself silent, feeling Tate's strength at my back.

I finished and looked up, and the horror in Tate's eyes had amplified. I strained my ears, praying to every god, known and unknown, that my men would be here soon.

Because Lacy was sobbing, the man, the monster, was panting heavily, and Edon was calmly, softly trying to soothe Lacy.

"Look away, little one," he whispered on a jagged inhale, as if in pain. "Close your eyes and plug up your ears. I'm alright, ok? Everything is going to be just fine. Can you sing me that song; the one you taught the children in the school? Just close your eyes and sing and I'll be able to hold you soon."

"You promised me a good fuck," the man grunted, his voice ragged and filled with violence. "Not a limp body and whining."

"I'm sorry, Master," Edon said gently, and then there were wet sounds and soft gagging, and I couldn't hold back anymore.

I issued out orders and they were followed silently. I couldn't sit back and let the man I loved be raped as I listened helplessly. And from the way

Robert and Tate, Nibley, Dasan, Cain, and the rest of my men watched me as I ordered them into position, I knew they understood.

And they were behind me.

29- Dirty Secret

✱ *TRIGGER WARNING**

EDON

The man's cock was thick in my mouth, his smell rancid and sour. His hands were everywhere, his teeth biting and drawing blood. His dry fingers were pressing inside of me, three at once, as I tried not to vomit on his dick.

I glanced over at Lacy whenever I could and was relieved when she remained curled in a ball, her hands clasped over her ears and her face buried in her knees. She had sung for a few minutes, but her voice was trailing off now and I knew she had to hear us. The wet slaps of the man's skin against my face as he thrust his cock into my mouth. The gagging I tried to keep quiet as he forced himself down my throat. His panting, wheezing breaths as he opened me up for him.

At first I tried to picture Lhiam as I sucked the man down. Tried to imagine that it was him holding my body, preparing me gently for his entrance. Tried to imagine that I was giving Lhiam pleasure with my mouth. But every time the man thrust inside of me, and I tasted my own blood dripping down my throat from his violence, Lhiam's image shattered and I was alone on a bed that smelled of blood, and I was again a dirty whore for a man to use.

The man finally pulled his cock from my mouth and I hastily grabbed his wet cock, pressing him to my entrance, and began to bear down on it.

"Good boy," he growled, biting my nipple harshly and drawing a sob from my throat. "Such a good cock slut for me."

I felt blood trickle down my ass as the man pressed himself past the first ring of muscle, but then, just as he sighed in pleasure, he jerked, yanking from my body. And then he was gone, and I sat up, confused.

The man was on the ground, surrounded by his quickly pooling blood. Tate was lifting the still-sobbing Lacy into his arms, his hooded eyes dangerous, and Lhiam stood above the man, his chest heaving, his body covered in blood. It dripped from his hair, his armor, and the huge broadsword he was pulling from our attacker's body.

"Edon," he groaned, and then I was wrapped in his cloak and then his arms, and I felt my entire body give out as I melted into him.

"Lhiam," I sobbed, digging my face into his chest. He held me so tightly it was almost painful. I felt a small trickle of blood drip down my throat, and another down my thighs. "I'm so sorry, Lhiam. I didn't... I didn't know what else to do. I had to... to protect Lacy, I had to—"

"Gods above, Edon," Lhiam growled, yanking my body up so I was straddling his waist, my legs wrapped around his back tightly, as he continued to hold me to him. "Stop fucking apologizing for sacrificing yourself and saving lives!"

Lhiam turned with me in his arms, ducking out of the tent and stalking up to Tate and Lacy. Lacy caught sight of Lhiam and ran at him. Without letting me go, he pulled the girl into a half-hug.

"Thank you, Lhiam. Thank you, Edon!" she was whispering, over and over, her face pressed against the cloak that covered my body.

"Why the hell were you outside of the castle in the middle of the night, Lacy?!" Lhiam yelled as he finally let me down so he could grab Lacy's shoulders. I could feel and hear the men around us gathering up the bodies of what I assumed were mercenaries or robbers, but I tuned them out.

After everything, I was back to where I had been.

"You not only put yourself in danger, you put Edon in danger! You both could have been killed, and Edon had to—" His voice broke, and I had to pull away from his embrace when he tried to reach for me again. He glanced my way, but he seemed content that I was still beside him because he turned his attention back on Lacy.

"I'm sorry, Lhiam," the girl sobbed, but I gently grabbed Lhiam's arm. He turned to me, concern and fear heady in his eyes.

"It was me," I whispered. Tate, Robert, Nibley, Dasan, and Cain all stood around us, trying not to look like they were listening, but staying near in case there was further danger. "Lacy was just following me. It's my fault."

"Dammit Edon," Lhiam hissed, his frustration now directed at me as Lacy sobbed even harder. Tate held the girl against his chest, his suspicious eyes on me. "What were you doing in the middle of the night? If you're going to run around at night, at least—"

"I wasn't ru—... I was leaving, Lhiam. I was leaving the keep, and Lacy followed me."

Lacy hiccupped, and I could hear heartbreak in the sound. But what hit me harder was the look on Lhiam's face.

Confusion turned to frustration, then to realization and when the pain visibly hit him I almost doubled over as the sight nearly took me to the earth. And the smell as he took a step back, his eyes shading, darkening, his right hand clutching the armored tunic at his chest, made me dizzy.

I had never smelled pain so potent.

"You were leaving me...? Last night... that was you saying goodbye...?"

When his hand jerked up, almost seemingly involuntarily, to reach for my face, I flinched and hoped he didn't notice. I wanted so much to push myself into his arms, beg his forgiveness, and let him take me back to his room. Enfold me in his warm, safe arms, and never let me leave.

But the feel of his skin on mine in that moment would have been torture. Especially with another man's bite marks covering my body, blood trickling slowly down my thighs, and the taste of pre-cum and blood still on my tongue.

And with the knowledge that it would again be the last time I felt his touch.

Of course he noticed.

His face hardened, his eyes narrowing as he clenched his fist and dropped it to his side. "I had no idea my touch was so abhorrent to you. Why didn't you tell me? I never would have...!" His voice broke, and horror wafted off of him, along with the smell of bile as it rose to his throat. "All of this time... everything we did...Was it because you felt sorry for me? Because you felt indebted to me? Did you want any of it?"

I won't be a kept whore; a dirty secret, I wanted to say, but I kept my mouth shut. I couldn't say it. I wouldn't let myself be weak in front of him. I had to be strong. Because I didn't know if I could deny him if he asked me to stay despite my pain.

When I didn't answer, Lhiam's eyes darkened wholly, and his lips thinned. His hands clenched into fists, and a dark sort of calm came over his body.

"At least come back and get treatment for your injuries. You're injured," he said, his voice devoid of emotion as his eyes raised above my head. As if he was finished with me, and he wouldn't deign to look at me anymore. "Please. I promise you won't have to see me. I'll stay away. Just come back, heal, and we'll make sure you're properly provisioned for—"

Before he could say another word; before his words could rip out any more of my heart; before he could convince me to come back with him, where I knew I would never again have the strength to leave the man I loved, I let his cloak drop, leapt into the air and shifted on a run.

As I dove into the brush around the campsite, my heart burst at Lhiam's voice, calling out my name with desperation.

30- My Heart, My Soulmate

L HIAM

I made it back to the keep only because Robert held the reins of my horse the entire way back. I was almost surprised to feel my heart still pounding in my chest. I didn't know someone could survive with it beating so brokenly, with its pieces shattered and bleeding inside of them.

I had thought he had reservations. I had thought he was afraid because he was young and everything was new to him and his past held him back. But I hadn't ever really doubted his feelings. Especially not since the first time we made love in my room. Not since that first time he opened his body to mine.

Gods, how wrong I had been.

Not only had Edon never loved me in the first place, he had merely been putting up with me. He had endured my affection, my touch, because of... what? I still didn't understand. Pity, or gratitude for saving him. It boiled down to those options, and both had me wanting to spew everything in my stomach across my horse's back. I had taken a boy who had never really known love, family, a gentle touch, freedom, and manipulated him into a sexual relationship, convincing myself he felt things for me, and then pushed him to the point where his only option was to run away from me in the middle of the night.

But there was no mistaking that last night, with his thick knot filling me as he claimed me for his own. What had that been, if not some semblance of feeling?

Days went by, and I knew I was acting ridiculously. I had known the boy for a few weeks, a little more than a month at most. No matter what I convinced myself I felt for him, it wasn't possible. Because love couldn't exist only one way. Love had to be mutual, or it wasn't truly love.

I kept to my room as much as possible, although I rarely slept, a bottle of rum continuously beside me by the fire as I stared into it, tears pouring down my pathetic face as each of my dreams of my imaginary future with Edon went up in the smoke of the flames.

Each future kiss. Each future moment of bliss as I woke to his stunning face in the bed beside mine. Each breath of laughter as we lay in each other's arms. Each vacation, with our adopted children, little boys and girls brought into our makeshift family and cared for and loved and protected by a man and a wolf.

I avoided Tate and Lacy, because I knew both would have words of comfort or condolence, and I couldn't bear to hear either. I left my room only to attend council meetings, and even those I barely spoke and I listened not at all. Stefan convinced me to entertain the visiting princess, although he had to remind me of her name seven times before we even reached the garden. I went only because there was no reason for me not to. After Edon, I wasn't sure if I could ever fall in love again, so I had myself almost convinced that I could marry the woman just so I wouldn't have to deal with my damn councilors and their damn demands.

When I moved into the garden, the same one I had brought Edon's cage to the first day I met him, the same one we had first made love in, where I had first kissed him, I almost lost my breakfast. But I held it in, bowed to the woman, and then tried not to stare at the tree where I had leaned back as Edon thrust his body against mine and brought us both relief.

I didn't even remember our conversation, but I know I angered the woman. Probably with my silence and refusal to even look at her as I stared at the tree and thought of Edon's body writhing above me, discovering pleasure as he bit my neck to keep from screaming his orgasm to the heavens.

Lacy managed to track me down after a few days— weeks, maybe? I wasn't sure anymore. It was only after I had broken down in front of a group of people that she came to find me. I had been wandering back from the garden with the princess, my mind on the bottle of rum next to my fire in my room. And the children from the school ran up to greet me.

And Tay, the child Edon had taken such a strong liking to, ran up to me, grabbed my legs, and happily began babbling.

"Doggie! Doggie! Where doggie?"

I could feel the tears pouring down my face, but I couldn't stop them. I shook my head, gently pried the child from my knees, and escaped as quickly as I could.

Lacy found me staring into the fire, the empty bottle of rum at my feet, another half full on the table beside me.

I could hear her words, but they weren't processing. I turned from the fire, from the images of Edon dancing in the flames, taunting me with the unanswered questions he had left behind. With the knowledge that I was no better than any of the other men he had been forced to endure throughout his short life.

"Lhiam, you're scaring me, please!" Lacy's voice cried, and suddenly her tear-streaked face was there, right in front of me.

"Lacy," I whispered, my voice hoarse.

"Lhiam, Edon is gone, but I'm still here. Edon left us both. He was my friend, Lhiam. Don't you leave me, too. You're all I have left."

I stared into the girl's eyes, barely registering that she was crying her heart out, her little hands clenching my fists in her own, rubbing them as if to warm them. The ring I was clutching in my hand, the ring I had carried with me for days, scratched at her and I knew she knew what it was.

"He was... he was my heart, Lacy," I gasped, feeling the hot tears scorch down my face. "He was my one and only. I can't... I don't know how to live without him. I'm afraid he was the only one... my soulmate."

Lacy sobbed, digging her face into my palms, nodding silently. "I know. I know, Lhiam."

"How do I live when my heart doesn't work right anymore? How can I continue to breathe when each breath is this painful? How do I go on, when he took so much of me with him?"

"Lhiam, I'm sorry. I'm so sorry."

"Why didn't he love me, Lace?" I gasped out, the words burning on my tongue. "Why couldn't he love me?

"I hurt him. Why didn't he just tell me he didn't... he didn't want me? I would never have... I have nightmares about how he must have felt when we were... when he was with me. I can't even sleep for them. Lace, I'm a monster. He didn't want me, and I pushed him. I forced him—"

"— No, Lhiam," she hissed, slapping both of her little palms against my cheeks and forcing my eyes to her. "I can't pretend to understand why he ran. I don't know why he didn't choose to stay. But you are a good man, Lhiam. And you would never force someone that way. He wanted you, or he would never have— "

"It was all he knew, Lacy," I growled, knowing this wasn't a conversation I should be having with the girl. But she was so smart, so mature, and I knew her knowledge of the world would probably anger me if I knew its extent. "It was all he knew, and I made him feel indebted to me. He felt he owed me— " I gagged, close to vomiting up the nothing I had eaten.

Which made me realize I couldn't remember when I had eaten last. Gods I must look a sight.

We were interrupted by Robert and Cain knocking and coming into the room without waiting for either of us to answer.

"Your Highness!" Robert gasped excitedly. "Edon! Nibs and Dasan found him in the woods outside the keep, near Lake Sixmore. He's injured, sire."

The relief was only outmatched by the agony as I stood and, Lacy clutching at my hand, made my way down to Gerard's study.

31- The Ring

E^{DON}

The dreams may have been the worst part. They always started out beautifully: Lacy and Tay playing in the garden, the toddler chasing Lacy as a puppy clambered at their feet. Lhiam stepping up behind me, planting a gentle kiss against my neck as he whispered his greetings softly into my ear.

Lacy and Tay would run up to Lhiam, Tay crying out "Papa! Daddy, Papa's home!" as he launched himself into Lhiam's arms.

I would smile at Tay's exuberance and lead them all inside, with Lhiam's arm around my waist, towards dinner in our big, private family dining room.

And then the dreams would change. The foreign princess would bend down, pick up Tay, and the child would call her mother. Lhiam would pull himself from my arms, pushing me back into a dark corner, and kiss the princess. He would rub her pregnant belly as they laughed.

And then there were the dreams where I was my wolf, standing by Lacy's side as Lhiam and the princess exchanged vows, promising to love one another and be true. And after the ceremony, Lhiam would corner me in a dark closet and bend me over and fuck me, leaving me covered in his cum, dirty and sobbing as he left me alone again.

Those dreams were the worst ones. Not the ones seeing him with his wife. The ones where he was with her, and then he was fucking me hard and rough, in a closet, a chamber pot room, up against a wall in a dark corner, leaving me dirty and alone in the dark. The dirty secret he couldn't let anyone know about as he returned to his wife and children. I woke to those in my human form, my wolf's heart too weak to withstand the physical ache of my heart breaking.

I wandered aimlessly, sleeping only when my legs would give out, drinking and eating only enough to keep myself going. I was too weak to hunt, so I ate a few berries, some herbs I knew were edible, but otherwise I remained empty, hungry, and cold.

It was a few days before I realized I had gone in circles, and the smell of the keep hit my nose. I felt my entire body go taut, my heart hammering, as I began to run. There was no thought in my mind but Lhiam. I needed to see him. I had to.

He would take me back. I knew he would. He was too kind to turn me away. I would explain to him. I wouldn't tell him how I felt, because it would be hard for him to deal with a lovestruck freak by his side, but I would beg him to let me stay by him. I would be his pet. He would never have to see Edon the man again if he asked. Or I would be his whore. I would let him have my body, my soul, my heart, because I had thought I could be without him, and I had been wrong. Being his whore, at least I would be able to see him and love him quietly, in my own way. At least he would be mine, for a little while every few days. He would be mine, for as long as he could be away from his family.

I snuck past a few familiar guards, but when I made it to the south garden, our garden, and saw Lhiam there with her, I heard something inside me break off and I wanted to laugh at my own stupidity.

If my belly wasn't so empty, I would have hacked into the bushes. As it was, I forced myself to turn and slink back out to the forest. Back out where I belonged.

I was a fool to think I could endure that. I wasn't strong enough to watch them together for even a few seconds, much less over a lifetime. And I hadn't missed the silver, glinting ring in his hand. He was playing with it, twisting it around his fingers, as he watched the light play off the metal.

No. I couldn't think about it. Because the thing that had broken inside of me throbbed each time I thought of the silver in his hands, and the way she laughed as she brushed her fingers across his hand.

I wandered further this time, my mind completely empty. I was thirsty, hungry, and then I wasn't. Everything began to fall away. I slept more, but when I woke I didn't stop to eat or drink, I simply moved on.

By the time I noticed the bear cub, and smelled the markings of his mother all through the woods I was tromping through, it was too late. The agony of her claws tearing me open was almost a relief as a yelp slipped from my muzzle and I fell to the earth.

I prayed my end would be quick, but gods, I welcomed it. It was so quiet, so warm, and I would have smiled if my wolf muzzle could make the move.

But then both bears were gone, and I smelled two familiar men. I wanted to beg them to leave me, to let me fade away because it hurt so much less than that broken emptiness inside of me, but I couldn't form the words.

"Little wolf? Is that you?" Nibley called, just as Dasan cursed.

"It's him. Edon, hang on, alright? We're gonna get you home, little one."

I wanted to beg them to leave me, to let me bleed out in peace, and dear gods, not to bring me back to the keep. But the instant Dasan's hands began lifting me into his arms, agony speared through my body and I knew only black.

When I woke, it was to familiar scents and noises. Gerard's soft voice whispering reassurances. The stink of medicines, herbs, and the sterile, clean smell of the doctor's office. I could smell Nibley and Dasan, and Tate and Lacey. Although they were no longer in the room, they had been recently. Robert and Cain stood nearby, near the door I guessed, and Lhiam's scent came from the warm body mere inches from me.

I kept my eyes closed, terrified of opening them and seeing him. I didn't want to see him. I couldn't. I had to leave. Damn meddling humans. Why couldn't they have let the bear have me? I had been so close to freedom.

I don't remember going back to sleep, but then the next thing I knew I was waking again, with only Gerard by my side. He was asleep, thank the gods, snoring loudly, so I managed to silently stalk around him. Every move showed me where I ached, but I was healed enough that the gashes wouldn't bleed. I grabbed a cloak, and a pair of breeches that were a size too small from a drawer beside a bureau full of healer smocks. I donned the clothes and then made my way through the halls silently. Escaping would be so much easier if I could shift into my wolf, but I was too weak yet.

I made it to the southern gate, where I knew the change of guard would leave a blind spot for a few minutes.

I had made it just past the gate when Lhiam's cold, almost cruel voice rang out from behind me.

"You're nothing if not consistent, little wolf."

I froze, hearing the anger in his voice, the frustration, and the pain.

I was hurting him again. Because I wasn't strong enough to be what he needed, I was hurting him.

I vowed then and there that this time, I would make sure that he never had to see me again. Either I would seek out the highest cliff I could and leap from the top, or I would simply keep walking until my body gave out. But one way or another, I would never again bring pain to Lhiam because of my weakness.

I turned, flinching as I caught sight of him. Gods, he was a mess. The stubbled beard on his face was thick and days old. He smelled of rum, salty tears, and fire smoke. He smelled of desperation and hopelessness. His clothes were wrinkled and hung wrong on his body, like he had lost weight. His hands twitched and fiddled with something that flashed in the low moonlight, drawing my eyes.

The wedding ring. Why did he still have that? Why wasn't it around the princess's finger? Why was he tormenting me like this? He must know how that would hurt. Was he doing it on purpose, to punish me for my weakness?

"This ring belonged to my mother. And my father's mother before... The gods only know how long it has been in my family."

His voice was so quiet, so hesitant, I had to lean in to hear him. But that same voice brought about the emotions I dreaded. I felt safe. Secure. Wanted. With just those few words, I was drawn to him.

He was more dangerous to my sanity than anything I had ever come across. But I couldn't turn away. I would let him have his say, tear me down with his words if he needed to, and then I would make sure my own weakness never hurt him again.

Permanately.

"When I was a child, my grandfather used to tell me about the way he proposed to my grandmother. He had this whole romantic dinner planned, near the pond in the east garden, where she liked to feed the birds. He ended up knocking her into the pond, falling in on top of her, and losing the ring in the mud. It took them an hour and the help of three servants to find the ring. My grandmother would always say it was the most romantic proposal she'd ever heard of.

"My grandparents always wanted more children, a big family, but after she had my father, my grandmother got sick and never really fully recovered. They were... My whole life, I've envied their love. The marriage they had, filled with so much love and laughter and joy. The way they spread all that goodness around to everyone they knew... it was always something I just knew I would someday have.

"And I thought I had found that with you." His voice broke, and I closed my eyes as I began to smell fresh tears drop from his eyes. "I had all of these plans. Selfish, I know, to make plans for a future you couldn't ever want... But I had all these plans, these dreams in my head. The children we would love, the days spent with you by my side, the nights spent in each other's arms..."

He broke off, his hands shaking before he clutched them together, holding the ring between them, and then he shook his head and looked up at the moon above us.

"I can't, Lhiam. It hurts too much," I whimpered, clutching at my chest as that damn broken bit began to fly at his words. And I knew he believed them, but all of those things would only be possible part of the time. The majority of his time would be spent being the high ruler of the realm with a wife and children by his side. And those times where I was left alone would kill me so, so slowly.

"I know, little wolf," he whispered, his eyes bright as he smiled at me brokenly. "I only wanted you to know that no matter what, so long as I live, you have a home here. I love you, and I only want you to be safe and to be happy. I'm sorry that you weren't happy with me. But in the short time I had you by my side, you made me... so, so happy, my love."

When my sobs dropped me to my knees, I could see Lhiam take a step forward, as if to reach for me, before he pulled back into himself. I bent over, clutching my chest as pain rocked through me and I finally came clean. I finally told him my truth.

And I could only pray he would accept it and not ask me to stay, because I knew I could deny him nothing.

32- This is It

L HIAM

His broken sobs were tearing me apart, but I held myself in check. He didn't need or want me. He needed to be free of me. And this goodbye I had planned for him was meant to free him, to let him know he was loved, was worthy of love, so he could move on.

He clearly hadn't been taking care of himself over the last few weeks anymore than I had. His skin was pale, his eyes sunken and dull, with heavy purple underlining them. I could once again count each of his ribs, as they stuck out of his skin visibly, and his hands shook with hunger.

I was about to turn away, leaving him and my heart in the dirt behind me, when his broken words met my ears and I froze.

"I'm so sorry, Lhiam. I can't be your dirty secret," he whispered, the words sounding as if they were dragged from his very soul. "I tried. I even came back, but seeing you... with her. I can't. You can't... you can't ask that of me."

I turned back around, wanting to drop to my own knees at his confusing words.

"Edon, who? Who are you talking about? What secret?" I gasped as a picture began to form in my head. One so ludicrous I feared it just might be what he was thinking. "You think the entire castle doesn't know that I'm madly in love with you? You think they didn't know from the moment you arrived that I was wholly smitten?"

His sobs quieted for just a moment as he looked up at me, and then he was shaking his head, his chapped lips bleeding as he worried at them with his teeth.

"But Lhiam, Stefan and... and that princess. I saw you with her. And I saw the ring."

"My family wedding ring? You thought... You thought I was going to give it to her?"

Even for the moment I had debated marrying that woman, I had known she would never wear my grandmother's ring. No, in my mind, it would belong to Edon for the rest of my life, even though he would never accept it. It was his anyways. Because my heart was his anyways, whether he wanted or accepted it.

"Edon, I would never give this ring to her, even if I did, unholy gods not willing, marry her. I pulled the damn thing from the treasure room after..." I paused, unsure if I should continue. "I brought it out of storage after you let me inside of you for the first time, after you were injured to protect me. I wanted so much to give it to you. To ask you to be mine, but I feared... You had been through so much, and you were only just discovering yourself. You had only just found your freedom. I didn't want to take that away from you, but I also wanted to spend the rest of my life with you."

Edon was silent so long, I feared the conversation was over. His questions had been answered and he could move on. We had both found some bit of closure. But then his hesitant, wet words made me want to yank him into my arms.

"You were going to ask me to marry you...?"

"I was. I was worried about it, because I feared you would decline it. That was why I kept waiting. But then you made love to me, or, at least, what I thought was you... That doesn't matter now." I sighed, shaking my head and trying to forget the night he had shaken me to my core, and then a day later, no, hours later, finding out it hadn't been to him what it had been to me. For me, it had been a new beginning, a moment that I thought our feelings had finally found their way to each other. For him, it had been his way of saying goodbye.

"The moment you pressed yourself inside of me I thought: this is it. It's always going to be him and no other. And then you were gone and I was left with only half a soul and a shattered heart."

"Lhiam..."

"No. It's ok. I'm sorry, I'm not trying to press myself or my feelings on you. I just want to be sure there are no misunderstandings, and I never want to lie to you. I never had any intentions of marrying the Princess of Namase. Not until after you left and I realized you had taken any hope of a future with you, so I figured why not her? But she never would have worn this ring. It was always meant for you, and I would see it on no other."

"Lhiam..."

"I'm tired, and I'm cold," I cut in, terrified of his words of rejection, tender and compassionate as they may be. Because my beautiful wolf could never cause me pain on purpose. "I'm going to go inside. Goodbye, Edon. Please be safe, and I hope you find your happiness. Please be at peace, little wolf."

"... Is there no way you can forgive me, then?"

His words were so quiet, I was terrified I had misheard him. But when I looked down at him, on his knees ten feet from me, I could see the dark need in his eyes.

"Forgive you, little wolf? You've done nothing that needs forgiveness. You are a free man, and you're exercising that freedom. You owe me nothing, and you never have. It hurts me that I ever made you feel as if you owed yourself to me."

"No. No, Lhiam... Can you forgive me for allowing my past, my fear, and the words of others to overshadow my love for you? Can you forgive me for leaving you before you left me, so it wouldn't hurt as much? Can you forgive me for lying to you?"

I ignored most of what he said, not able to face the majority of his words. I could latch onto only the last few words that had left his mouth.

"When did you lie to me?"

I hadn't even realized it, but I was moving towards him. And before I knew it, I was kneeling in front of him, my hands clenched in my lap so I didn't misunderstand and reach for him again.

But the fire, the pain, and the burning desire in his eyes couldn't be misunderstood as he stared directly into my eyes and poured his vulnerable heart out for me.

"I lied by omission every time you spoke your words of love in my ear and I remained silent. I lied every time you spoke of the future and I didn't speak of my own dreams of a future with you. I lied every time you looked at me and saw a man who wasn't hopelessly in love with you. I love you, Lhiam. My soul loves your soul. My mind, your mind, and my heart..." His voice cracked. "My heart doesn't beat right if you aren't holding me in your arms. If you'll have me, an orphan freak without a name or a penny to his name, with a broken heart, a shattered soul, and a dark and dirty past, please let me spend the rest of my life proving to you how much I adore you."

His words washed over me like a soothing balm. My hands began to shake, sweat dripping down my spine as I stared into his beautiful, soul-rich eyes. He had poured his everything into his words, and my confusion was still heady, but I was beginning to understand his motivations. He had been led to believe that in order to be with me, he would have to accept a life of secrecy, a life where he was my kept plaything. With his past, I wasn't surprised that the idea had hurt him so much. And I wasn't surprised he had believed it so readily.

I only wished he had told me of the fears so I could have squashed them as the worthless thoughts they were. I had always meant to love him, to claim him openly. I had never intended to hold back my devotion and love from him.

I leaned forward to grab Edon's hands, clasping his shaking fingers between my fists.

"I'm going to speak plainly and without artiface, because we have allowed our fears and insecurities between us for too long.

"Edon, I forgive you everything in the past, and anything in the future. My heart is yours, and you may do with it what you will. Will you marry me? Please be my husband, and let me reward you for trusting me with your heart. Let me spend the rest of my life finding new ways to make you happy. Let me give you half of my soul, half of my heart, so yours can heal whole."

Edon's sobs amplified as I gently slid the little silver circlet on his finger. It fit perfectly, of course, because this man was always meant to be mine. And I, his.

"Love me, Edon. Let me love you. That's all I'll ever ask of you."

"I..." Edon began, and then he was nodding furiously, and his face was pressing against my chest. "I love you so much, Lhiam. Too much. It hurts to love you this much."

I wanted to laugh, because I knew just what he meant.

I pulled him from my chest only enough to press my lips to his, and it was like coming home. Like finding peace after a storm. Like the beginning of a million kisses to come.

I pulled Edon to his feet, dragging him into my arms and walking the few feet to the gate. His legs wrapped around my waist, his hard cock pressed up against my abdomen, as his mouth devoured mine. He tasted of tears and hunger and joy.

And gods, he tasted like hope. And like Edon.

I never thought I would ever taste him again.

His tears continued to fall, but I knew they were no longer tears of hopelessness. They were tears of joy, and I could feel my own eyes prick with the ecstasy and absolute joy that was rolling through my veins like fire.

"Love you," I growled against his lips as I slammed his back against the keep wall, using it as leverage so I could hold him still against me. I rutted against him, drawing whiny cries from his throat. "You and no other. Openly and fiercely for the entire world to see. Please never doubt that again, little wolf."

His nod was furious, his hands gripping my hair as his hips thrust against me, begging for friction on his cock. I worried for a moment that his injuries would open back up, but when I fingered his chest, where he had been all but cut in half, there were only raised welts that were almost completely healed.

"I'm alright, Lhiam. Want you. Need you. Please, my love."

His begging had me pulling his body down so our hips were joined, and then I was thrusting against him so our cocks were aligned. We could come once out here so our minds were clear to make it back up to my rooms... Our rooms.

And I would spend the rest of the night, and as many days as it took, showing his body that he couldn't live without me. Not anymore.

A subtle, embarrassed cough sounded from my left. I pulled away from Edon's lips just enough to glare down Nibley and Dasan. Both looked terribly uncomfortable, but they held their ground.

"You alright, little wolf?" Nibley asked, and I looked down into Edon's eyes. He was all but drunk with passion and lust, his hips still unconsciously jerking against me, his eyes glazed, and tears still dripping down his face.

I looked back over at Nibley and Dasan, and I saw the moment both men saw the ring on Edon's finger. They were discreet men, so I knew they wouldn't talk, but it was still disconcerting for anyone to find out before I had been able to tell even my councillors. Or Lacy.

"I'm..." Edon began, his voice cracking. He dug his face into my neck in embarrassment, and to my horror, his sobs amplified. "I'm so happy," he finished, to my relief. Dasan and Nibley were old friends, but even they would kick my ass if they thought I was hurting the man.

"That's good, kid," Nibley laughed, and then he clapped me on the back and Dasan laughed at my obvious discomfort. "Congrats on taming the wolf, Your Highness."

I chuckled and shook my head, dropping a chaste kiss to Edon's forehead as his tears continued to wet my neck.

"I didn't tame him. He just accepted me as his pack, is all."

I pulled away from the wall, resigning myself to walking with Edon clinging to me like a tree he was climbing. But Nibley's next words had the man in my arms jerking up straight.

"Hey Dasan, maybe you and I should've stayed quiet, let them go at it against the wall. Pay the little wolf back for his voyeurism."

I laughed all the way back to my room after Edon jumped from my arms, shifting in midair and landing as a wolf, yipping in irritation once before disappearing into the keep. Dasan and Nibley's laughter followed me until the castle doors slid shut behind me.

33- Yours. Always.

E^{DON}

I waited semi-patiently for Lhiam in his room. I thanked the gods that Cain was his guard tonight, because the man barely spared me a glance as I snuck into the room. I feared if it had been Robert or Tate I would have received the third degree before they allowed me in.

I only had to wait a few minutes before Lhiam was crashing through the door, and then I was on him. I couldn't get enough of him. His taste, his hot skin against mine, his smell. Gods his smell was intoxicating.

I dragged him back to the bed, ripping his clothes from his body as I shoved him back onto the cushions. I reached over, grabbing the oil from the drawer beside the bed. After yanking my own sparse clothes from my body, I straddled Lhiam's thighs, my hips thrusting the empty air, as I set the oil by Lhiam's head.

Lhiam fingered my lips, his eyes wet with gathering tears. "I thought... I thought I'd never see you again. I thought you were lost to me."

I froze above him, staring down into the eyes of the man who had rescued me, saved me, who loved me, who I couldn't live without, and I smiled with every bit of myself I could.

"It tore me apart to... when I left," I admitted.

"I'm so sorry that I didn't ensure that you knew my feelings, my intentions. I'm so sorry—"

"— No," I whispered, my fingers on the prince's lips to quiet him. "No more apologies. No more pain. Please, Lhiam, please let me show you how I love you."

Lhiam's entire body tensed up, his mouth going slack as I bent my body to take his hard, leaking cock into my mouth. I pressed it back as far as could take it, my tongue laving against the thick vein that ran up the length of his engorged member. He cried out, his hips jerking as he tried desperately not to thrust into my mouth. I wanted so much to give him this, this pleasure he had given to me without question so many times. But I needed inside him. I needed it like I needed my next breath.

Pulling away, I lathered my fingers with the oils, and opened his body to me gently, my fingers shaking as I stared into his eyes. He watched me with an intensity I wanted to lose myself in, holding his thighs up and spread apart to give me easy access to his body. His fingers dug into his skin so hard they were white with the strain.

"I love you," he whispered, his eyes fluttering as I added a third finger, gently rubbing against the insides of his body and shuddering as I remembered knotting inside his tight heat.

"I love you, Lhiam. So much," I gasped, pulling my fingers out and sprawling my body over his. He let his legs fall around me, wrapping me in his warmth, his feet digging into my ass as I humped my hard cock against his.

I devoured his mouth again, thrusting my tongue against his and tasting him like the most decadent meal.

"Show me how much," he moaned, lifting his legs again and smiling coyly. "Show me how you love me, little wolf."

I pulled back only enough to position my cock at his entrance, and then I was inside him and groaning as I pushed as deep as I could. Lhiam hissed and arched his back, his eyes slamming shut as he cried out.

"Edon!" he whimpered, and I shut my eyes, reveling in the feel of his body clamping down on mine. "Edon, move! Oh gods, move inside me, my love!"

I obeyed, thrusting in and out as gently as I could, my rhythm as steady as I could manage with my entire body taut and shaking like a leaf in autumn.

"I'm not going to last long, Lhiam," I whispered, leaning down and licking and sucking at his lips as my thrusts deepened and quickened. "Need you too much. M... mine."

"Yes, Edon; yours... Always. Come inside me, little wolf. Make me yours."

I reached down, grasping Lhiam's cock and grunting in satisfaction when he immediately stiffened in my arms and I felt his hot, wet release coat both of our writhing bellies as he groaned his pleasure. And then I was coming, my entire body jerking and my scream piercing even to my own ears as my knot tugged at his rim once before I embedded it inside his body, tying us together, my hips flush with his ass, my back arching as I released myself inside of him.

"Oh gods, Edon, I can feel it— I can feel your cum so hot inside me. Fuck, your knot presses right up against my prostate, little wolf. Feels so fucking— ugh!" Lhiam's body jerked and his face contorted beautifully as he came again, his fists clutching the sheets by his head and his back arching up towards me. Gods, he was beautiful when he came.

I froze in Lhiam's arms for a few minutes, just reveling in the tightness around my body and the feel of his hands stroking my hair back from my face, but soon I noticed Lhiam's cock was still hard against my belly. I looked down into his amused eyes and growled in pleasure as he rocked his hips up against me and gasped at the move.

"Oh gods," he whimpered, his fingers digging into my upper arms as I humped inside him gently, not wanting to hurt him, stirring my knot against him as much as I could. It was an incredibly tight fit, but I could manage a few inches of movement. And I began a very slow, steady thrust of my hips against his ass as Lhiam's eyes widened and he shuddered.

"Make love to me again, my love," he whispered, pulling me tight and biting at my ear to spur me on. And I complied, feeling as if my body had been made to pleasure his.

34- Stuck

L HIAM

When I came back down for what felt like the dozenth time in a matter of hours, Edon was still inside of me. I felt another spurt of his cum hit my insides and an agonizing aftershock spread through my limbs. After discovering he could still move, even in small increments, while knotted inside me, Edon had spent the gods only knew how long showing my body the pleasure his could bring. But now he was engorged bigger than I had ever felt, and I knew we both needed a break or he may never be able to pull himself from my body.

Not that I would complain if I had to live my life tied to him, but it may be a little inconvenient in many ways. Reality was painful like that.

I moaned, my entire body shaking as Edon twitched on top of me. "Try to hold still now, my love," I whispered desperately. I didn't know if I could handle another orgasm. But when he was inside me like this, it was like they were squeezed from my very soul, even if my body couldn't handle it.

"I'm sorry, Lhiam," he whispered against my chest. "I don't want to hurt you."

"Gods, sweetheart. It's the farthest thing from pain. Only a little over-whelming."

He nodded but stilled when I gasped as the move jerked my body. I chuckled, rubbing my hands up and down his back. I kept my legs locked around his back, my ankles wrapped around each other at his ass, to try to keep him pressed against me as closely as possible so his knot didn't drag against my sensitive rim or swollen prostate.

The knock at the door startled us both, as did Robert and Tate entering without any other warning. I noticed that neither seemed surprised to see Edon, so I assumed they had spoken to Dasan and Nibley.

I dragged a blanket up and over Edon's exposed ass, growling at the two men as I cupped Edon's ass over the blanket possessively. I received only amused looks and an answering growl of approval from Edon.

I looked over and was amazed to see that the sun was beginning to rise outside the window. My gods, how long had Edon been fucking me?

"I suppose congratulations are in order?" Tate asked as he moved to stoke the fire in the hearth. He kicked at the three empty rum bottles on the floor. I hoped Edon hadn't seen them, but one look up into his shining, sad eyes showed me he had.

"It doesn't matter anymore. You're here now." I kissed his nose gently, and he dug his face into my neck, still so careful not to jostle me.

I turned to the two men. Robert was studying us with amusement, and a bit of confusion, his eyes roaming our joined bodies beneath the blanket, and Tate seemed to not even notice the state we were in as he stoked the fire and then settled himself in one of the armchairs facing the hearth.

"Would you give us a minute?" I grumbled in annoyance. "Or... a few minutes?"

"From the sounds through the door, you were both finished... again. I don't see the problem," Tate answered, rolling his eyes as he glared over at me.

I could feel Edon's embarrassment rush through his body, and he didn't seem to be able to stop from squirming to try to dig his body further against mine. Robert's eyes on us were discerning, and I wondered how much longer it would take for him to figure it out.

I gritted my teeth as Edon's squirming tugged his knot against my hole and I ran my fingers through his hair, trying to calm him.

"It just... I'm... we're a little stuck at the moment. Can you just give us— "

"Stuck?" Tate grumbled, standing and moving over to the bed, his hands on his hips as he glared down at us. "Just pull it out, Your Highness. If it goes in, it can come out. We have things to do. You should tell Lacy yourselves or she's never going to forgive you for letting Nibley and Dasan be the first to find out."

Finally, I could see understanding dawn in Robert's eyes. Along with a heady amount of amusement.

"Oh my gods," he gasped suddenly, his eyes shifting from me, lying on my back with my legs wrapped around the smaller man in my arms, to Edon's hips glued to mine. He watched the way neither of us moved, despite the embarrassing situation, and he guffawed.

"Like stuck stuck?" He whistled, and I saw Tate begin to comprehend as well, because his cheeks flushed as he stared down at my raised legs and the embarrassed, horrified boy in my arms. "You go, wolf boy. That's an interesting bit of anatomical information I'd just love to hear more about."

I rolled my eyes, but Tate was already moving towards the door. He grabbed Robert, who followed seemingly reluctantly.

"You could have just said the wolf knotted you, Your Highness. We'll go," Tate grumbled, drawing a whimper from Edon.

"Is it really so big it won't come out, even if you try to— "

"Robert!" I snapped, amused but annoyed on Edon's behalf. The poor man was trying to make himself invisible in my arms, his face digging into my neck and his breaths hot against my sweat-soaked skin.

When the men were gone, I drew Edon up to face me and chuckled when I saw his blood red skin. He was blushing all the way up to the tips of his ears.

"I'm so sorry, Lhiam," he whispered, shaking his head in horror. "Now they know that you... that I... that you let me..."

I laughed, shaking my head and pressing kisses all over his red face, and then over his ears.

"Don't apologize, my love. I like that your body knows I'm yours. I like that it mates me. It shows me how you really feel. And the fact that others know I belong to you, body and soul, is not something I will ever be ashamed of, little wolf."

———————————————————————

We bathed together, exchanging one more gentle orgasm with hands and lips and tongues, before I helped Edon to dress and then dragged him to the throne room. I had sent a message with one of the servants who set up our bath for Tate to gather the councilors, Lacy, and any other courtiers in residence in the keep.

When we neared the room, Edon froze, and I knew he could hear the crowd in the room and I would need to explain before moving forward.

"My love," I whispered, pulling him around to face me and cupping his face in my palms. "Those people in that room— they need to know that you're mine, and that I'm yours. We have to tell them. Fuck them and what they think of us; but we have to tell them, so they know where I stand. You're my fiancé, the future husband of their prince, and I will not tolerate disrespect towards you."

"Lhiam," he mumbled, his cheeks going blood red as he bit his lip. He fiddled with his tunic, refusing to meet my eyes. "I'm not... I'm an orphan with no name, no money, nothing— "

"You have the heart of a prince," I answered as I leaned down to kiss his lips with the barest touch of my own lips. "And that is more than most of them can lay claim to. Besides, you are also one of the wealthiest people in that room now, next to Lacy and me, since everything that is mine is now yours. My love, my heart, Edon, please remember that I love you, and nothing else matters."

He nodded, and I could see him gathering himself. Then he met my eyes, smiled, and grabbed my hands in his.

"I'm ready, Lhiam," he said, his voice quavering only slightly as he straightened and slipped a gentle kiss onto my jaw.

35- Partner and Lover

E^{DON}

My anxiety had hit a whole new level as I stepped into the throne room, with Lhiam clutching my hand in his own. I wanted nothing more than to shrink back, hide behind him, shift into my wolf and run away with my tail between my legs.

But Lhiam deserved more from a mate. From a lover. A partner.

He deserved a strong, courageous husband who stood beside him. And gods help me, I would be that husband if it killed me.

And from the glares I was getting from Stefan and a few of the other men beside him, I thought it just might.

When Lhiam reached the throne, he turned to the small crowd— many of which I recognized, some I didn't— and held our joined hands up, the ring glinting brightly on my left ring finger.

"Ladies and gentlemen, thank you for coming. I would like to introduce to you my fiancé and future husband, and your future Prince Consort, Edon Wolfe."

I almost choked at the ridiculous surname he had given me, but the smirk on his face told me he was finding far too much amusement in the name.

There was silence in the room, broken only when a squeal of excitement broke through the crowd, and then Lacy was all but tackling me, little Tay and a few other children close on her heel.

How had she even snuck them all in?

I returned her enthusiastic hug, pulling Tay up into my arms as well, holding his excitedly squirming body as tight as I dared, just as one of the men I recognized took a step forward.

"Your Highness," Rafael said firmly, his voice carrying through the hall, as I'm sure he intended. This was the man who had been one of only a few threats the time Lhiam had brought me with him to a council meeting as a guard.

He now watched me with knowing eyes and a hint of a smile in his cold, stoic eyes.

"I think I speak for the majority of your people when I bid you congratulations on your engagement. May your marriage bring you and Mr. Wolfe many years of happiness!"

A few murmurs of agreement filled the room, until there was a loud clapping starting from where I could see Dasan, Nibley, Robert, Tate, and a few of the other men I had spent time with in both my wolf and human forms. Even Cain met my eyes, nodded, and his lip twitched in what I assumed was a possible smile.

I had never been this happy. I felt accepted, loved. Wanted.

But the child in my arms demanded my attention, grabbing my hair and yanking hard while he cried out, "Daddy! Doggie, Daddy!"

I dug my face into his hair, holding him to me as he clutched me back, and whispered into his ear so softly, praying only he heard.

"I'll never let you go, little one. I promise. You're safe now. You're not alone anymore. I'll take care of you."

But when I looked up at Lhiam, meeting his eyes with a hint of trepidation, his smile lit up my chest until I could feel nothing but his love and devotion.

His kiss over Tay's head— over our son's head— was so tender, so gentle, I felt tears dripping from my eyes. And the rest of the world seemed to fall away as we were soon surrounded by friends and well wishers. And the few who opposed our joining were forgotten in the midst of the support and happiness we were overwhelmed with.

Epilogue: Wedding

EDON

Our wedding was as small as we could make it, with it being the wedding of one of the high rulers of the empire. The emperor, whom I was horrified to find was a close friend of Lhiam's— they had played frequently as children together, Lhiam told me— attended. His being there made it possible for us to only invite him, and not every other ruler of the different realms of the empire.

"If I'm here," he told me, his beautiful hazel eyes shining with mirth as he stood far too close to me, drawing a glare and a growl from a fuming Lhiam. "Then I'm the emissary for the empire, and you need no other."

Only our friends and family attended the wedding. Tate stood by Lhiam's side, Cain by mine. Lacy walked me down the aisle to my love, and brought us the rings. Lhiam's had been made to match mine, the swirling silver gorgeous on his thick, strong finger.

Cain and I had become close over the few months while we prepared for our wedding. It started when he came up to me during Lhiam's announcement of our engagement. He congratulated me, in a language I recognized like a memory from a dream. And the answering words fell from my lips, in that same language, faster than I could notice that I was speaking a foreign tongue.

I had stared, shocked, at Cain's harsh but knowing face, as he bowed and then straightened and shrugged.

"I had guessed, Prince Consort," he said as I felt dozens of gazes fall on us in shock. "But I hadn't felt it was my place. Forgive me if I overstepped."

Since then, we have spoken many times of our shared homeland— a far away country he called Akar, where the men were fierce warriors, the families were large, and what he called the wild magic was powerful.

I guessed he had a secret he had yet to share with me, something about the wild magic, which he said was the reason I shared a soul with a wolf, but I wouldn't push him. I had come to know the closed-off man as much as I could, and I knew he would tell me in time. And nothing I could do or say would push him into divulging sooner.

The animosity between the emperor and Cain was marked from the day the outgoing, sensual emperor leapt from his horse, landing in front of a stone-faced Cain, and planted a full kiss to the other man's lips. After a shocked moment, Cain shoved the taller man back, wiping at his mouth, and spit on the dirt at the emperor's feet.

My fear had been great, terrified the emperor would order Cain arrested, but the man only guffawed and shook his head as he put his long, smooth fingers to his lips and smiled seductively.

"Such a spoil-sport, Akaran," the emperor said with a heavy, purring rasp. "This is a time of love and beauty. Let me love your body, beauty."

Cain's annoyance was held in check with only clenched fists as he stood solidly at attention. "No thank you," he said simply.

The emperor's laughter was like the rushing of wind through trees as he bowed a little and turned away. "I'll change your mind, beautiful Akaran. Mark my words," he all but giggled, finally moving to Lhiam and me. Lhiam was keeping his laughter in check only by biting his lips between his teeth, but I was horrified.

This was the emperor of the 7 realms? This flighty, flirty, absolutely stunning man, that had even me blushing as he looked me over and smiled in the same way he had when openly looking Cain over.

The emperor stayed only a week, a few days before our wedding and a few days after. I rarely saw Cain during that week, as he spent most of his time hiding from the pursuing emperor.

I was coronated Prince Consort the day after the wedding, with the emperor presiding, and only two days later we officially adopted Tay.

And had plans to adopt many, many more children. As many as we could, to fill our home with the love I had never had, and that Lhiam had in abundance to share.

LHIAM

After the public announcement of our engagement, Stefan and a few other councilors cornered me, demanding I take back the announcement and break the engagement. To take a wife, and keep Edon as a concubine only.

I did what I should have done years before.

I gave Stefan and the three councilors who always backed him an ultimatum: retire and return to their own homes, or I would force the retirement on them and they would lose the chance at the honorable way out.

I assured Stefan that the only reason I was being this merciful and not imprisoning him for the pain and suffering he caused to both me and my lover was because said lover had begged on his behalf.

He hadn't wanted any kind of animosity to darken the beginning of our life together.

But I swore, if I ever saw him again, I would ensure he was arrested for acts of treason. That I was essentially banishing him to his small, northern castle.

They all chose the former, and within days I replaced them with Tate, Robert, Dasan, and Lacy.

Needless to say, the first female councilor to the prince, and it was a pubescent female at that? Two more councilors quietly moved into retirement, and I was able to replace them with two nobles I knew wouldn't be afraid to stand up to me, but wouldn't have their own interests in mind when dealing with matters of state.

One of which was Lady Sera, a sweet, quiet, but fiercely passionate woman who had been born a man, but since a very young age had dressed and acted as a woman. And now, very few even knew that she had ever been anything but Lady Sera, daughter and heir to Lord Spencer.

The only problem I could see with the arrangement of two women on the council, was how very smitten Lacy seemed with the beautiful Lady Sera. But I was assured quickly by both Edon, and Lady Sera herself, that my cousin was only young, and would get over the infatuation.

I honestly didn't know how I would react if she never did get over it.

The day of our wedding was, of course, the happiest of my life. Watching Edon move towards me, his tunic, shirt, and pants perfectly tailored to his stunning body, I was struck dumb. Riece, the emperor, was behind me, whistling softly in admiration as I could only try to keep breathing. Even as he held my hands in both of his, Riece's words marrying us floating by my ears, I was unable to hear anything past the pounding of my heart in my ears.

Until Edon said, "I do," and kissed me, and the world came back into color and sound. And the laughter all around me at my deaf and dumb state washed over me.

"Well, Your Highness?" Edon whispered, his eyes lit with laughter as he shot a look at a doubled-over Riece. "Do you take me as your husband?"

"Dear gods," I managed to hiss out on a breath. "I do. Always, until my last breath takes me, I'll choose you, Edon."

THE END